ECHOING YESTERDAY
Volume One in the continuing story of
    the people of *The Island*

Tragically orphaned when a storm at sea claimed the lives of
her parents and baby brother, Clemence Kinrade was given a
home by her uncle Jesse, whom she loved dearly—perhaps
too dearly. When Jesse took a wild and wanton Irish girl for
his bride, Clemence, growing to womanhood felt the sharp
pangs of jealousy. But handsome, menacing Luke Karran
was soon to occupy all her thoughts. Luke, son of the
black-eyed Johanne, thought by many to be a witch, was
driven by dark and destructive urges . . .

At the Midsummer Revels Clemence, emboldened by a love
—philtre, meets Luke in a passionate encounter—but when
she finds she is with child, Luke is cold and distant, his
affections by now elsewhere . . . until the night when he
walks with Clemence on the treacherous Chasms . . .

ECHOING YESTERDAY

Volume One in *The Island* series

ALEXANDRA MANNERS

CORGI BOOKS

ECHOING YESTERDAY
A CORGI BOOK 0 552 12084 7

First publication in Great Britain

PRINTING HISTORY
Corgi edition published 1983

Copyright © Alexandra Manners 1983

This book is set in 10 pt. Palatino

Corgi Books are published by Transworld Publishers Ltd.,
Century House, 61–63 Uxbridge Road,
Ealing, London W5 5SA

Printed and bound in Great Britain by
Cox & Wyman Ltd, Reading

FOR KELLYS EVERYWHERE

PROLOGUE

The storm came out of nowhere. Afterwards, islanders maintained that an unnatural stillness had fallen just before the gales.

Lily Kinrade had no such premonition. She cuddled Sammy who was fretful with the pain of his first tooth and watched the firelight flicker against the ceiling in patterns of cream and rose. How like Joseph he was! The thought of her husband filled her with pleasure.

Into the quiet of the September night crept a tattoo of discord. Soot fell into the hearth and the woman gasped as the acrid sourness caught at her throat. The baby coughed and struggled in her arms.

'There,' she whispered. 'There. You'll wake your sister. 'Tis only the wind in the chimney.' But she shivered suddenly as the gale hit the roof with a great bang and a slate slithered to crash into the street. The baby cried out in fright and she held him closer.

'What is it?' Clemence asked out of the darkness.

'A bit of a breeze,' Lily replied with deceptive calmness. Her heart had begun to race. Her Joseph was out there in the unexpectedly hostile blackness. He and many others were fishing off Clay Head. The night had been clear enough when the boats went out.

More soot clattered down the chimney, obscuring the small fire. The coloured patterns faded from the low ceiling and a tense dimness settled over the room. Clemence climbed out of the wall bed she shared with her mother when her father was at sea. Going to Lily, she sat close beside her. 'Dada,' she said, voicing both their thoughts. 'Dada will be all right?'

'Of course,' Lily said mechanically. It was expected of her to show optimism in the face of fear.

The girl crept even nearer, the warmth and familiar smell of her mother's body a bulwark. Little Sammy, undeceived by Lily's show of bravery, began to howl in earnest as slates continued to fall in a salvo of gunfire.

Lily rose to light a candle, the child held against her breast. His strong little hands clutched at her hair as every window in the house rattled. Other windows showed lights as townsfolk were aroused by the ferocity of the wind.

Clemence remembered every tale she had heard of bugganes and phynnoderees, glashans and water-horses. Every story of witches and malevolent beings.

The wild sobbing around the eaves was accentuated and the girl shivered inside the white calico night-gown. The fire was smoored and her mother chilled and rigid. She recalled that there had been an inexplicable mist over Douglas that afternoon, a grey pall that had changed the narrow streets to shiversome canyons.

'Mannanan,' the woman in the baker's shop had said, looking over her shoulder, and then she had murmured something about the giant who was held in the underground maze of Rushen Castle and who periodically escaped to throw a cloak of cobwebs over the island or such portion as he thought fit. There were huge footfalls in the sound of the tornado.

Something grated and tore across the roofbeams. A great "crump" echoed against the cobbles. Someone screamed. Lily ran towards the window. Pale candle-light showed women struggling to keep their shawls about their shoulders and old men staggering and clutching at walls and door latches. The shrieking tempest cast leaves and dust into every face.

Many people were already running towards the harbour, torches streaming in wild golden ribbons.

8

'Stay here, Clemence,' Lily ordered in a strong, hoarse voice. She was flinging open the door and Sammy's yells were part of the night and the echoing clatter of pattens against the rounded stones. Yesterday had been so different, autumn sunshine, Joseph laughing and holding her close, making irreverent jokes and discussing what they would do next week. Next year—

Sobbing, Lily followed the other panic-stricken figures. Somewhere at the back of her mind lurked the realisation that she had not waited to protect herself or the baby from the piercing sharpness of the night air. She had left her daughter in a room where the fire still smouldered. But nothing seemed to matter except the fact that her husband was at the mercy of a sea that could drown him.

It was her fault for laughing at the stories of Mannanan. Joseph said that the mists were only the results of heat and cold. But he was as godless as his father. Old Samuel had turned against religion when his wife Sarah died. In old Bishop Wilson's time it was. Sarah was a mute who had somehow displeased the Bishop; he had it in his head that she was dim-witted and rebellious. He'd had her dragged behind a boat as a punishment. The sea was supposed to be a cure for idiocy. But poor Sarah drowned and Samuel had rejected Christianity, as did Joseph when he was old enough to understand.

Lily ran towards the anaemic light that marked the entrance to the harbour.

* * *

Joseph Kinrade could see the pale glow at last. The sail was a black, flapping shape against the sky. Most of the lanterns had been cracked and broken, leaving the sea a nebulous enemy. Only the harbour light held out hope.

It seemed hours ago that the devil wind had struck, tearing at sail and net, spilling the sea across the bows

9

to gather in acid lakes about their feet. Bob and Jackie had been baling ceaselessly while the rest were at sail and oar, hanging onto a useless rudder, praying into the rampaging squall. The creaking violence was rent by cracks and shouts, the plunge of a body into the waves, despairing cries.

Joseph's face was raw with the sting of salt and wind. The mast groaned. Another lantern was doused and the shape of Man moved suddenly upon them, a long sprawling substantiality that spelled danger. The gale whipped through his thick garments as though they had been paper.

He thought of Lily and his children. They were the closest he'd get to futurity since he'd rejected God. Joseph was aware of a sick certainty that he'd not see them again, then repudiated the weakness firmly. He saw his daughter's face, all pallor and fairness like the picture of an angel. A cry tore at his throat and was carried away on the voice of the gale.

The mast creaked again and gave a harsh, final crack. The spar shuddered and toppled and the sail enveloped Joseph like a huge, sodden bat. He heard Jackie's muffled shouts and the hoarse terror gave him the strength to fling off the heavy folds and emerge, still upon his knees, into the frantic air.

Joseph felt about him and jabbed his fingers against splintered wood. He called upon his companions but there was no answer.

Crawling in deepening water, his hands encountered something cold and yielding. He felt jerseyed shoulders and a limp head. Lips still faintly warm. The head lolled upon a broken neck.

The bucket bobbed towards him and he began to scoop at the water. There was a dreadful rhythm to the movements. All around him there was a sinister activity. Boat struck boat, men cursed and were swept away to cling briefly to spars and wreckage. Some distance away a spilled lamp had set fire to a wherry. The sea was bloodied.

Joseph saw the light at the harbour's end, pale as a

mirage, then a great bulk came between himself and it, crushing into the timbers. Half-stupefied he was thrown into the water, his mouth filled with stinging salt. The boat, black against the flames of the burning wherry, rocked close by him. 'Help!' he shouted then clung to a plank, retching.

A rope snaked wetly out of obscurity and struck Joseph hard across the cheek. His eye hurt abominably as the end of the line flicked across the eyeball, but he grasped at the rope and was jerked towards the side. Tears forced themselves from under the damaged lid. Blinking and breathless, he could just make out the Douglas light, unreal as a glow-worm.

Lances of fire ran up into his forearms and wrists. His shoulders protested. Joseph struck the rescue vessel and was, for a moment, half-submerged. There was a grasp at his hands and he was pulled then dropped on to hard boards. He lay there for a time, his face bruised and nose bleeding, half-aware of the activity around him. Shouts, grunts and panting breath. The wet squeak of a thick rope. Feet that passed and repassed.

Sick and dizzy, Joseph heard someone cry out that the harbour light was only a quarter of a mile off. No one mentioned the rocks. He struggled to his feet and was thrust against the mast but his fingers slid away from the polished wetness. He tried to focus his eyes.

'Lily,' he whispered. 'I've tried. Tried to get back to you—'

The wherry had burned out and trailed red feathers over the sea until the waves reared up against it, hissing angrily. In a few moments the smouldering remnants were doused.

Joseph, nauseated by the smell of fish and the raw smart of the injury to his eye which he feared was bleeding, staggered to the side.

The Douglas light was still there, a Holy Grail. If he got back safely, he'd never repudiate God again and if he did not— He tried not to think of the latter. Someone must earn Lily's keep and his children's. He

11

must be there to see Clemence grow up. She was such a frail little creature.

The thought of his mother Sarah obtruded. Sometimes he had the fancy that she'd tried to lure him to join her, like a mermaid in search of a human soul.

A great cry broke from him. The beacon was gone and the air was rent with the faint screams of women. They mewled like gulls, ineffably sad. It was his useless eye that made him think they were abandoned on a sea pounded by a banshee wind. But all the men were shouting now, fear battering behind the hoarse entreaties, the disbelief, the curses.

Swept onwards through the maelstrom they saw nothing but the implacable outline of the island only a fraction darker than the sky. But there was no escape from the sounds, the sea-bird grief of wife and lover.

The foremost boats hit the rocks and the breakwater. Joseph was aware of an impact that jarred him to the roots of his teeth. Blood poured from his bitten tongue. He tried to speak and could not. There were only ugly, guttural moans that made him think fuzzily of Sarah who had not been able to answer the Bishop. He tried to evoke the image of Lily but she would not come to him.

'Clemence?' he whispered but her name was destroyed in blood. He was propelled into a great wet mouth that chewed and mumped its toothless gums upon all his limbs. Reaching uselessly for anything that had survived, he touched only a flaccid body that nudged him in sickening familiarity.

The wave swallowed him as he flinched in revulsion and threw him on to rock that bored into his head. His blood ran unnoticed in the dark.

* * *

Clemence took her cloak off the peg behind the low door. She had put on her stockings and pattens but had not waited to change into her daytime clothes.

The wind tore at her nightgown as she joined the

trickle of people who had not yet arrived at the harbour. There was no moon, only the faint wash of lamplight on the cobbles. A slate skimmed past her head and split itself against the surface of the street but Clemence hardly noticed under the stress of her anxiety. Someone shouldered her aside and she was thrown against a projection that bit into her knee. Crushing back the inclination to cry, she set her teeth and stumbled on.

The night became unreal. Dervish leaves whirled and beat against her face and they were real enough. But the groaning figures that surrounded her in shadowy phalanxes bore no resemblance to the people she knew. She told herself that this was a nightmare from which she would presently awake, but the pain of her grazed knee impressed itself on her consciousness and she knew it was fact.

She summoned up her father's likeness and was sick with fear for Joseph. The dark handsome face with its ruff of beard and sparkling, hazel eyes would not be exorcised. She loved him terribly. Her happiest moments were when she was allowed to creep into bed beside him when Lily was elsewhere. His body was so strong and warm and his beard tickled her so that she would laugh with a pleasure she could not explain. Sometimes it seemed that she was jealous of her mother.

Clemence repudiated the thought as she found herself behind a great rampart of Douglas folk, mainly women, jamming the way to the harbour. Again she was aware of the cold fear that washed around her stomach and set her shuddering. Her mother would never have left her without good reason and that reason must be Joseph. Clemence wondered why he had gone out if a storm was coming. But he could not have known. The weather was perfectly normal earlier apart from Mannanan's mist. Did the giant really haunt the dungeons of Castle Rushen?

All the noises of the dark rushed upon her ears like an answer to her question. It was not an ordinary

13

night. The battering gale was filled with reminders that life was threatened by the unforeseen. In that moment she believed in all the dread creatures of Man. Who else could have conjured up this terror?

Desperately, she tried to convince herself that all was not as bad as it seemed. She pushed at the ranks of sturdy thighs and hips that blocked her way, but press as she might she made no headway. Mingled with the smell of wool and fur and sweat was the scent of fear.

Though she had glimpsed the light of the Douglas beacon on her way here, there was no sight of it now. But Joseph would see it. He was too good a seaman to founder on his way from Laxey.

'Mama,' she said aloud. 'Mama?'

The stout calves against which she had been thrust stood aside to let her through. Some distance off, a pink glow died slowly. Against it she saw profiles that stared blindly and lips that moved. Figures genuflected and were still. Someone keened softly.

Now that she was at the front, she could see the light again. She stared around her for a sight of Lily. In the distance a child had begun to cry. Clemence battled her way towards the sound but it was not Sammy, only an older, uglier infant taken there because it could not be left at home.

Suddenly, she could not see at all. Women screamed as the waiting figures were plunged into darkness.

'A mast struck it. Struck the beacon!'

'They'll not see the way. Christ Jesus!'

Bodies pressed forward and Clemence clung, limpet-like, to the nearest leg. She seemed to be on the edge of an abyss. The air was filled with wails and oaths and she had an inclination towards vertigo.

There was another cry that was like Sammy's. Clemence heard it above the snapping and cracking from the rocks.

'Joseph!' That was her mother's voice.

Clemence clawed at the stout belly and surprisingly small shanks that blocked her way.

14

'What's this, then?' The voice was not unkind.

'Let me past, please!' Her urgency had the desired effect. The legs shrank away to leave a space just wide enough to allow her passage.

'Joseph.'

'Mama!' Clemence cried out. 'Where are you?' Her fingers fastened on voluminous skirts. Not her mother's.

'Clemence? Is that you?' Lily's voice had sharpened. She sounded quite close.

Sammy cried again and Clemence strained her ears to discover their exact position.

Something was happening. There was some sort of altercation. Lily cried out 'Don't push me! It's my little girl. I must find her. Stay back.'

There was a scream that Clemence was always to remember, then a violent splashing and thrashing from the sea. Sammy's wails cut off in midstream. People gasped and pushed forward then stood silent. But the noises from the sea went on for some time as Clemence stood frozen, great hands pressing into her shoulders so that she could not move.

She did not hear her mother any more. Perhaps Lily would not have fallen into the sea if she had stayed at home as she had been told.

Suddenly Clemence was beating and scratching at the arms that restrained her.

* * *

PART ONE

CROGGAN

CHAPTER ONE

Clemence came to herself in darkness. She tried to go to sleep again but excitement gripped her. It was market day and instinct told her that the fine weather of yesterday would be repeated.

The first pale streaks of dawn showed her the now familiar surroundings of her Uncle Jesse's cottage. Up here, on the sleeping-platform, all was still cast in deep shadow, but through the wooden bars she could make out the pale rounds of the plates on the oak dresser and the dim mass of a table and bench.

Below her, Jesse was snoring.

She lay for a time, savouring the present and the promise of the future. How long it seemed since the tragedy of losing her entire family in one night.

The Christians from whom Joseph had rented the tiny house had taken Clemence in with them. Liza Christian was good-hearted and took care of the child's material wants until her relatives could be summoned from Croggan and Peel. Like Liza, Clemence's mother had taken in visitors during the holiday season, supplementing Joseph's earnings from the fishing. They could not otherwise have managed.

Clemence had eaten without noticing the taste of the porridge, herring and oatbread washed down with buttermilk. The sharing of the Christian children's bedroom was of no account. She was divorced from the whispers and chatter, the stifled laughter from under the bedclothes. Mr. Christian did not need to farm or fish. The house was large enough to take in many botanists and walkers and college professors from Britain, holidaymakers from Lancashire and Galloway.

Though she had asked to, Clemence was not allowed to go down to the harbour where the gruesome aftermath of the storm was still cast up on the rocks.

Aunt Deborah had been first to arrive. She was tall and thin, like a birch planted on insufficient soil. Eyes, skin, hair, all reflected a luminous neutrality. She was absent-minded to a degree and there seemed little warmth about her. When she embraced Clemence, her arms felt like willow branches.

Clemence heard the young Christians whisper that Deborah Quine was a witch and a flicker of interest had stirred inside her. This had vanished with the appearance of Uncle Jesse Kinrade. He was so like Joseph that her heart opened out to him and the tears she had so far repressed came flooding out. Her grief spent, she sat red-eyed and quiet, watching his brown face in the firelight.

The subject of her future was introduced.

'She can stay with me,' Aunt Deborah suggested.

'Oh, I want to go to Uncle Jesse!' Clemence said quickly.

'I've nothing fancy, child,' Jesse told her kindly, 'and there's no woman in the house. You'd be better off with your aunt.'

'I'll take care of you. Mama taught me lots of things.'

'But why?'

'Because you look like Dada.' It seemed good enough reason.

'I'm not him, though.' Jesse had looked a little uncomfortable.

'But—if Deborah doesn't object—'

'I've no objections.' Deborah had broken a piece of oatcake with birdlike fingers and Clemence was suddenly aware of the pale eyes drawing her own into a strange uncomfortable stare that seemed to last for ever. Perhaps she did mind.

'She can always visit you,' Jesse said, ruffling his thick, dark hair that was so like Joseph's. Clemence had experienced a stab of pain that was almost pleasure.

'Aye, she can do that if she's ever the need or inclination,' Deborah agreed, and just for a moment her eyes were blind and pearly as pieces of honesty, seeming to swallow the bitter, hurtful part of Clemence and leaving her drowsy and uncaring.

So it was settled.

They found the bodies of Lily and Sammy the following day but Joseph had been swept away. Someone might find him on the Galloway shore or on Blackpool sands. Nearly everyone in Douglas wore crêpe.

After the funeral Jesse had fetched a horse that was small and sturdy with long black hair that tossed back against her cheek. He'd told Clemence its name was Fiddler, because the animal so enjoyed the jigs and shanties he played when he was not working on his holding at Croggan.

Clemence, remembering her far distant amusement, smiled again, noticing that the room was perceptibly lighter, recalling too how beautiful she had found the journey from Douglas to the cottage she now knew so intimately. The leaves had been turning colour, those that had not blown off in the gales, and she'd found the gold and yellow exciting against the flush of heather. There had been glimpses of the sea from the higher points and deep shadowy glens she'd wanted to explore.

In spite of the novelty, she had begun to tire long before they came in sight of Castletown. She was nodding with weariness but was not quite asleep because of the ache in her backside from sitting astride Fiddler. It was a change of sound from the diligent hooves that had jerked her to wakefulness. A rabbit fled from a barking dog. The low sun gilded the towers of Rushen Castle and turned the window spaces to strips of ink. Chimneys smoked peacefully though most of the house roofs had lost slates. A laden cart was silhouetted against the quayside.

Clemence had stared at buildings that were almost as high as the masts of the ships that clustered against the harbour wall, their sails the colour of rusted blood.

The horse picked his way between barrels and boxes. The fire of the dying sun and the red of the sails shivered in the water. Though Clemence had sworn never to like the sea again she could not help but think it beautiful.

Jesse told her that he had friends just down the road at Scarlett and that she could stay there for the night if she wished. She replied that she'd prefer to go on. Here and at Scarlett the sea would be all around them. At Croggan she need not see it unless she wished.

Past Ballacloole they'd skirted the Black Rocks and remembrance of her loss returned to weigh upon her spirits. She had made herself think of other things. How she would look after her uncle and, later, pay a visit to Deborah. The thin moon that coloured the water was the uncanny pallor of Deborah's eyes. Mesmerised, she'd allowed her heavy lids to close and was aware of Jesse's arm tightening around her waist.

Somehow, that warmth and proximity had been the beginning of the strong and lasting affection that coloured her life. The desolation of those first days, before she had adjusted to her new situation, and the knowledge that she would never again hear Sammy grizzle sleepily and Mama speak to him in soothing tones as she dealt so capably with the timeless chores of motherhood, had been eased by Jesse's unquestioning acceptance and cheerfulness. Although Clemence had loved her father best, she missed him less because her uncle was so like Joseph that it was, in time, as if she had not lost him at all.

And now she was fifteen and that lost, conscience-stricken child a ghost who came infrequently. Being fifteen meant that she was considered a woman, old enough for love and marriage. Already, Jesse teased her about this and it was not hard to realise who would be her uncle's choice of a future husband.

The fact that she had different ideas banished the pleasure of her unaccustomed lazing in the warmth of her cosy pallet. Clemence groped for her clothes and began to pull on the clean gown.

Jesse had risen and was going towards the dark mouth of the fireplace, yawning. A flitch of bacon swung, creaking, as she climbed down the short wooden ladder. That was intended for market. Islanders rarely ate their own produce. Butter, meat and fowls were for barter.

The light of the lamp flared just as she reached the floor.

'You should have stayed abed.'

'I'm wide awake.'

A black pot hung from a chain and the fire was responding to the bellows. Clemence knelt, stirring with the wooden spoon. There was a curious comfort in the homely task. In every house in the world it was necessary to begin the day in this fashion. She felt safe and protected from harm here with Jesse, and as yet wanted nothing to change.

Jesse spoke of ordinary things over the usual breakfast of gruel and buttermilk, and she was content to listen with half an ear to the timbre of his voice while her thoughts pursued their own course. Jesse's hair was still damp and his face shining from the wash at the pump. Affection stirred in her.

When he had gone to harness Fiddler to the sledge she seized the broom to sweep the hard clay floor, made the beds and rinsed the traces of buttermilk out of the bowls and the pewter mugs.

It was light enough now to see the massive roof-beam and the fishing-rod fastened against it, the creel and the bag made of suggane, the face of the grandfather clock whose slow tick accentuated the quiet.

She dusted the spinning-wheel and the two chairs, the small, scrubbed table, the green glass bottle that contained a tiny ship, wondering, not for the first time, how it came to be there. Then she turned out the lamp.

Clemence heard the sound of Fiddler's hooves and the excitement came again, more urgent than before.

She ran to the doorway and stayed there, outlined by the first, strong rays of the sun. The bright, harsh light turned her hair to pale fire and accentuated the jewel-like blue of her eyes. Even the faded forget-me-not of her gown was beautified briefly. Everything was burnished, the swaying trees of the copse, the glimpse of the stream and the wild flowers on the bank.

She ran her fingers through Fiddler's tough, wiry hair and suddenly, her hand was still. Luke Karran was watching her from the other side of the water and for a moment everything was frozen into a luminous tableau with his dark, gipsy face as the focus.

Even as a grief-stricken child, she had been over-poweringly conscious of Luke. She could never forget her first sight of him.

It was a temptation afterwards to say that she had known in that first moment that he would bring her nothing but harm. But hadn't she found Luke Karran's face exciting right from the beginning? Sullen and moody and dark-skinned. Black eyes and hair as shaggy as Fiddler's. Strong—

She had been instantly aware of her own extreme fairness and appearance of fragility. It was obvious she took after the Quines, though there was no weakness in Deborah.

The thin, blunt-ended lips had moved. 'Who are you?'

'Jesse Kinrade's niece.'

'Never seen you before.' He had come closer.

'I've never been here before.'

'Staying, are you?' The dark eyes were openly curious.

She swallowed. 'Yes.'

'Why?'

Was he being deliberately cruel? But she could not

24

run away from the question for ever. Others would talk about what had happened.

'I have no family. They were drowned.'

His eyes narrowed and there was a fleeting glimpse of recognition, quickly masked.

'Heard about all those men. But how did it happen your Ma died?'

Because I disobeyed her, Clemence thought, and a hot, acrid sourness filled her. I killed her. Killed Sammy. Her irises became so large that they had almost swallowed the thin, pale face.

'Throw herself in after him, did she? Wouldn't kill myself for nobody.'

'No, she didn't!' Rage had overcome every other emotion. 'And if you wouldn't, it's because you've no heart! No heart.'

He had laughed, half-admiring her show of courage, but obviously nettled by her assessment of his character.

'What's all the noise?'

Another shadow had lain across the green, a larger, broader shadow, and the husky voice was a woman's. 'Haven't you nothing better to do, Luke Karran?'

The newcomer was a female Luke, all darkness and gipsy eyes, her handsome face as fierce and sulky as his own. Clemence, struck dumb, could only stare at her.

Luke had removed himself just out of range of his mother's powerful hand. 'Told me I was heartless, she did.'

'Well, aren't you?'

'No.'

'Get yourself about your business, Luke.'

'Only asked about her mother.'

Mrs. Karran's gaze was only for Clemence. The girl had experienced the curious conviction that the woman could see Lily's body, limp and flaccid and bound with seaweed.

Clemence had never been able to forget the intentness with which Luke Karran's mother had received

25

the mention of Lily, or the dark cruelty that seemed the essence of Luke. But, though there had been no interchange of visits as there was with the Kinrades' only other neighbours, the Conroys, there had been a subtle build-up of the relationship with Luke. Clemence had never been able to fathom how Luke seemed able to gauge her movements when she was out alone, nor could she count the times her heart had almost flown out of her body when she had taken some turn of the path to find him obviously waiting. He would lean against a tree-trunk or a bit of hedge or wall and laugh at her discomfiture, his white teeth nibbling at a clover or a stem of grass, his black eyes roving over her body from head to foot.

Jesse disapproved of Luke as much as he disliked and mistrusted Johanne, the mother, and Aggie, the daughter. 'Bad blood in all the Karrans,' he'd said. 'Wild as heather and Johanne's got a reputation for witchcraft.'

There'd seemed no link between Johanne Karran and Deborah Quine who was also reported to be a witch. But women in country places were always suspect when they were out of the ordinary. There'd been an old body near Douglas—cross-eyed and reclusive. With a cat— They stoned her, left her half-dead.

The Karrans would themselves be going to market, Clemence thought, responding to Luke's sensuous smile, then turning away as Jesse came, his arms filled with provender to stack on the sledge. There was no point in rousing Jesse's suspicions at this tenuous stage. He knew nothing of those meetings. Clemence had told no one, not even Bessie Conroy, but treasured them in her heart while realising she must not take it for granted that Luke must one day love her. What one wanted and what one received were seldom the same thing.

Once the sledge was loaded, Clemence saw that Luke had gone but he would be there on the quay at Castletown, swaggering and grinning at all the prettiest girls. The Karrans' produce was never as good as

Jesse's or the Conroys' but the women swarmed round Luke like bees round one of his own honey pots. That was the only thing she disliked about market day.

'No time for day-dreaming,' Jesse said, not unkindly. 'See if Hugh's ready.'

She ran down the slope between the shining birch stems, balancing on the fallen trunk that had been placed across the narrow stream. Blue smoke twisted from the straw roof. Two hens and a duck scuttled outside as Clemence reached the open door of the Conroy cottage. Early as it was, the place was filled with the mouth-watering scent of bread and a savoury smell escaped from the big black pot that hung from the slouree.

Meg Conroy came out to greet Clemence. She was a pleasant-looking woman with a freckled face, always scrupulously clean. There was no problem that was too much trouble to Meg and the girl had been fortunate in acquiring this surrogate mother. Meg's daughter, Bessie, a plain, good-natured girl, had shared her adolescent dreams with Clemence.

Then there was Hugh. Clemence's mind stalled.

'Bessie's been taken badly,' Meg said with a pucker of worry. 'Stomach pains. So it's only Hugh today. Don't suppose it's anything serious but it's not like Bessie to ail.'

'I'll bring her something tomorrow.'

'That's a kind thought, lass. Ah, there you are!'

Hugh had come round the side of the neat dwelling with an armful of cheeses which he deposited on the step. The image of his mother, he had few of her go-ahead characteristics.

'We've been ready for ages,' Clemence told him as Meg disappeared inside the house.

'I'd best hurry, then.' Hugh smiled. It was a very pleasant reflex but it had little effect upon the girl. She had grown up with Meg's son and he was a kind of brother, part of the comfortable and undemanding background of everyday life.

Clemence missed completely the little spark of devotion in Hugh's grey eyes. He was somehow like a chair into which she fitted and could find rest.

But this was not the time for idleness. It was Clemence who saddled and harnessed old, white Bill to the Conroy sledge and fed him a carrot while Hugh busied himself loading produce.

Together, they led Bill up the slope to the wooden bridge where Jesse was waiting impatiently.

Clemence closed her ears against the two men's easy conversation as they passed the Karran cottage that was the antithesis of the Conroys' limewashed and neatly thatched home. Johanne Karran's domicile had a dirty, neglected look, brambles and nettles right up to the gloomy door and the sod roof weighted with rough lumps of stone. Odd plants grew in the tangled back garden and once Clemence had seen dull, purple berries that Jesse told her contained poison. Pods from laburnum lay drying on the grubby sill.

She had not seen Jim Conroy this morning.

Jim Conroy was a decent man who worked hard for his family but had not the charisma of Jesse. Clemence decided she would die quite happily for her uncle should there ever be the need. Slowly but surely she had become fitted to hold the reins of the Kinrade household in her small, pale hands. Meg had taught her to plait ropes of suggane, to wash clothes and to cook more than porridge. With Bessie she went to gather turf and ling and gorse to offset the mixture of turf and coal in times of need, to feed the poultry and make butter for market. She learnt to deal with fish and to skin and gut the occasional rabbit, to take honey from the hives on the moor, then make polish from the wax.

Meg's pride was her son Hugh. But he had his father's reserve and unswerving principles which made him, on occasion, dull in Clemence's opinion. She was always swiftly ashamed of the unworthy thought. Hugh worked uncomplainingly and was always considerate towards both his family and Clemence with whom he had endless patience. Still, it was

28

surprising how often she wished he would show some spark of wit or passion. Jesse could make her laugh over some amusing tale or other, and Luke—Luke had only to cast her a predatory grin that bared all his magnificent teeth and somehow draw his black eyes upwards into the wickedest slant and her body inexplicably ceased to be her own. He was hateful. He was violent. He was—Luke. Without him, her restricted, though mainly enjoyable world, would have been a less exciting place.

The heat of the sun was shut off as the sledges were drawn into the wood, bouncing on the dried mud of the well-defined track, the green shade cool and delicious. She swayed as their sledge slewed at the bend, and grabbed at the bacon flitch to save herself, but both she and the flitch were flung off into the ditch.

Breathless, she was pulled out by Hugh and lifted to her feet while Jesse scrabbled for the precious bacon. Clemence wanted to laugh.

'Are you all right?' The pressure of Hugh's fingers became painful and Clemence was aware of some strong emotion in his expression that made him almost a stranger.

'Of course I am. And you're hurting me,' she said sharply.

'I was afraid you might be injured.' He released her and now his face was pale. It was disturbing to realise the depth of his feelings. Clemence had never seen him as anything but a rather uninteresting boy. It was disconcerting to find that it was a man who faced her in the shifting shadows of the wood. That inclination towards hysteria ebbed away.

'As if a small tumble like that would be serious,' she scoffed.

'It might have been,' Hugh replied, obviously hurt by her ridicule.

'Well, it wasn't,' she said more gently and rubbed at a green mark on her skirt.

'Anything,' Hugh told her in a low voice so that

29

Jesse couldn't hear, 'that hurts you, hurts me. Surely you must know that?'

Clemence stared at him. This was something she had not bargained for. While she knew that Jesse approved of her friendship with Hugh, Conroy had been clever in that he'd never previously shown anything but an ordinary pleasure in her company.

'You mustn't think like that,' she whispered.

'Why not?' he asked.

'I don't want things to change. Please, don't try—'

'What are you doing?' Jesse called out. 'Come! We were late in starting anyway. Don't let's waste more time.'

'Sorry,' Clemence answered, glad to be separated from this new, perplexing Hugh. But at least she had had her wish! He had shown something more than dullness. Again, that bubble of amusement rose inside her. Not that it would get him very far.

Clemence had an overpowering image of a similar incident last winter when she'd frolicked on the snowy slopes with Bessie, the world a shivering magic of white and blue, and Luke had watched from the wood like a great creature of prey. He had laughed as she slid, screaming, into a deep gully under some purple thorns.

'Look out for him,' Bessie had advised, ignoring him, but Clemence had been unable to repress the hammering of her heart. That flashing smile had reminded her of a picture of a wolf she had seen at the Christians'. Danger was stimulating.

There was no such reaction towards Hugh who had behaved so differently. All of her senses remained unmoved except for a flicker of embarrassment. But, looking at him with fresh eyes as he guided old Bill along the forest track, she saw that even his figure had broadened and developed, unnoticed until this moment. It would be difficult to return to their former camaraderie.

It didn't matter, she told herself. She had all she wanted for the present. Jesse had become most satisfactorily hers to manipulate and care for, obedient to her every whim. He'd taught her to ride and groom Fiddler, to row the boat he kept down at Bay Stacka under the lowering regard of Spanish Head. She loved Jesse and he loved her. They needed no one else. Almost angrily, Clemence pushed away the treacherous memory of Luke. Not even Karran must come between herself and her uncle.

They reached Castletown early and set up the little stalls close by Castle Rushen. She could see the boats on the water and the stones of the castle reflected. There were dogs and children, sailors and fishermen, a pervading smell of herrings and tarry rope. The sea no longer intimidated her. To an island, the sea was everything. It gave the townspeople ship-building and net making, the shoals that fed not only Manx men and women but the slaves in far-off countries who were nourished mainly on the barrels of salt-herring. In Man it was a lucrative business. The sea brought visitors, naturalists. And the Irish in search of work.

There was a girl on the quay who was obviously Irish and down on her luck. The shabby clothes and down-at-heel shoes could not totally detract from the girl's looks. Clemence, seeing Jesse's intent stare, would not willingly admit to the attraction of a white skin and orange-red hair, outrageously large and dark-fringed eyes that knew too much for their own good.

The owner of Kerruish's boat-yard saw her too as he strolled along the quay with a big cigar, abstractedly puffing expensive smoke into the faces of passers-by. Barney Kerruish made no dramatic figure. He was frog-shaped but his face and his wide mouth were pleasant. His good nature, Clemence had already noted, made him popular enough with Castletown worthies. Even his innate shrewdness could not make him see that the immigrant Irish wench would be after one thing only, his money. He promenaded several times along the quayside instead of his usual once, and each time his eyes sought her out.

She, cunningly, seemed not to notice, and stood,

wrapped in a ragged shawl, the wind teasing at the mop of red-gold hair, her face white as alabaster.

Maddeningly, the girl stationed herself not far from Jesse's stand, every now and again allowing that black-fringed gaze to return to a scrutiny of Jesse's broad shoulders and rumpled curls, his easy jesting manner as he called his wares to the motley passers-by. Stout housewives in print gowns, and shawls in spite of the heat, came forward to prod the cheeses and inspect the brown eggs that were fluffed with small feathers. Jesse knew most of the women and pleased them by asking after their families.

'When are you getting wed yourself?' one old beldam in rusty black asked him.

Clemence held her breath. They shouldn't put such ideas in his head. It was bad enough pretending to be asleep when occasionally Jesse tiptoed into the cottage with someone like Molly Kelly. But to have Jesse married! She could not understand the lance of pain that thrust through her. Wasn't she having dreams about the Midsummer Festival? Dreams in which he could have no part.

'Tomorrow,' Jesse answered good-temperedly, 'if you'll have me.'

The old crone cackled with delight and pushed gnarled, ivory-yellow fingers through her hair in a pretence of titivation. 'I'll be at the church. Waiting.'

Jesse grinned and caught the eye of the Irish girl who smiled back at him, then tossed her red hair defiantly as a passing beggar reached out to touch her.

'Leave me be, you dirty beast!' she cried.

'Yes,' Jesse supplemented, coming round to the front of the stall and leaving Clemence unwillingly in charge. 'Keep your hands to yourself or I'll have to teach you your manners.'

The vagrant smelt of ale and other less agreeable things. His red-rimmed eyes, angry now, reminded Clemence of a pig's that had wallowed in muck. Long, black nails scratched at his rags. 'She—shouldn't,' he

pronounced in a slurred voice, 'be standing there
—then, asking for—trouble.'

'The only one asking for trouble is you,' Jesse told
him flatly. 'Get on your way and leave the lady alone.'

'Lady!' the man mocked. 'Lady is it! More like—'

He never finished the derogatory description that
hovered on his shrunken lips. Jesse took hold of him
angrily and propelled him along the dockside to thrust
him into a noisome corner, then returned briskly,
rubbing his hands against his breeches.

'Thanks,' the girl said and this time her eyes flicked
over the foodstuffs on the stall. 'Nice bit o' cheese that
looks.'

'Want a piece?' Jesse asked, his mind obviously on
other things. Clemence hated the way he looked at the
wench, his eyes travelling from neck to breast, then
discovering the line of her long legs as the wind blew
the threadbare skirt against them.

'Haven't no money to pay for it.'

'Take a slice, anyway.' Jesse picked up the long,
sharp knife and cut a generous wedge. 'Just off the
Dublin boat, are you?'

'That I am. There was nothin' there to keep me. You
could say I was asked to go.'

'The man who sent you across the water must have
been blind as a bat and with water instead of blood.'

'And you're not like that?' The girl smiled secretively
and nibbled at the corner of the cheese as if she meant
to make it last.

Perhaps she had to, Clemence thought, but the
flicker of compassion was doused when Jesse leaned
towards the girl and whispered in her ear.

'We've customers!' Clemence said sharply. 'Paying
customers.'

The girl laughed. 'Seems I'm distractin' you from
your work.' She shivered as a sudden thrust of wind
flattened the garments against a body that did not look
noticeably undernourished.

Jesse feasted his eyes for a moment, then the girl
moved away, her shoulders braced against the unex-

33

pected chill. Looking upwards Clemence saw a cloud obscure the sun, a cloud as dark as the weight on her heart. Jesse was frowning at her and Hugh was pretending, from the bulwark of his own stand nearby, that he had seen and heard nothing.

'She was begging quite openly,' Clemence said when the little rush of customers had gone with laden baskets. 'She was as bad as that awful man.'

'Just be thankful you've never been in the same situation,' Jesse told her more curtly than she liked. Tears pricked at the back of her eyes. Was he casting up his own generosity after her parents died? He wasn't like that, she acknowledged silently.

Jesse's reaction disturbed Clemence anew. He could not concentrate and more than once Clemence had to point out that he'd undersold some of the precious produce.

'What does it matter!' he'd been driven to expostulate.

'Of course it matters,' Clemence had returned in a hard little voice she hadn't known existed. What was wrong with her? She overcharged the next few items surreptitiously.

Later, Jesse sent her off to buy herself a bit of gilded gingerbread and a piece of blue ribbon and she forgot the coldness between them. She owed everything to her uncle, even this unexpected treat.

'Thank you,' she said gratefully.

'That's all right.' Jesse sounded detached and his mind was obviously on some other matter. She wished, futilely, that he'd seemed more involved but he was staring down the quayside at the gate that led to Kerruish's yard though there was nothing to see but a few joiners and riveters eating their lunch of oatbread and drinking ale.

However, the black cloud had moved on and the sun shone from a sky as blue as cornflowers. The warmth played about her body as she moved in search of the tiny bowfronted shop round the back of the castle. As she entered it, she thought how grand some of the big houses were on that rise, with trees around them and sparkling windows that looked out over the ships' masts towards the sea.

The gingerbread was warm and smelt delicious. She had intended to keep it so that it could be shared with Jesse but the combination of the sun's heat and the scent of ginger was too seductive. It melted on her tongue so that she had to keep on tasting and swallowing until it was gone.

She caught sight of herself reflected in another window. How tall she seemed and how slender. Her loosened hair swung whitely against her shoulders and she remembered the promised ribbon. The coins lay in her palm, inciting her to extravagance. It was a long time since Jesse had been so generous.

There was another reflection behind her own and she spun around, startled. Luke smiled down at her with the dangerous good looks of a satyr and all at once Clemence was dry-mouthed, her heart hammering. The white-toothed grin was both luring and repelling. He made her so aware of her body that it was quite indecent.

'Only pass the time o' day with the Karrans,' Jesse had cautioned when Clemence first came to Croggan, and common sense told her it was wise advice. But caution had nothing to do with muscular shoulders and sunburnt arms and teeth that gleamed against a man's dark skin. Such snares shouldn't be set for any girl. Yet the day would have been empty without a glimpse of him.

'You got a crumb on your lip,' Luke said softly. 'Shall I get it off for you?'

Clemence rubbed the back of her hand over her mouth with more violence than was necessary. 'There's no need to bother you. Let me pass. I'll be late at the stall.'

'No need to hurry, is there? Last I saw of Jesse, he was getting on fine.'

'What do you mean?' Again, she was attacked by nameless fears. That girl—

'Nothing that need concern you. Or us.'

'Us?' How hotly the sunlight struck her unprotected face. Her voice cracked foolishly.

'Don't say you've never thought about me. Seen you peeping over hedges and across between your cottage an' ours. You want me, Clemence Kinrade, don't you.'

'I don't!' It was more a cry for help than a declaration. He was much too close for comfort and she was out of her depth. One slightly dirty finger was tracing a line from her wrist to her elbow and her senses reacted strangely. She struck his hand away but it would have been so much more satisfying to let it remain. Now that it was gone she wished it back again. His shirt was open at the neck and her eyes were drawn to the gap. She wanted quite badly to touch the dark flesh inside it. Jesse would be so angry if he knew. She clung to the thought of him as a drowning sailor might look for a spar.

'Grown real pretty, you have,' Luke told her, making no move to let her leave the confined space in which she seemed penned by his tall broadness.

Did he mean it? She prayed that he did while the one sane corner of her mind told her she was a fool. There was nothing constant about Luke Karran. She'd seen him before on market days.

'Wish I could say the same about you.'

Luke laughed, seeming not at all disposed to let her go and a hot tightness came into her chest.

'You think too much of yourself,' she went on. 'Anyone'd think every girl in Castletown was set on you. Well, I'm not!'

'No?' The black eyes mocked her.

It was odd how she had always been able to talk to anyone except Luke. The childish repartee had none of the depth of expression she could have wished. How awful it would be if she could never say the right thing and she lost him to some cleverer, less involved girl here in the town. But none of the Castletown women had ever gone back to Croggan with Luke. And she was always there. The strength of any future relationship could lie in that proximity. No man lay in wait for a girl if he had no interest in her.

He ducked his head suddenly and his mouth covered hers. His body pushed hers against the low window so that the frame creaked alarmingly. Someone inside the house was shouting. Luke released her, laughing, and Clemence took the opportunity to struggle out of the circle of his arms and away from the displeasure of the irate householder.

'There was a little bit of gingerbread I missed,' Luke said.

Part of her wanted to laugh with him. The other half felt threatened and insecure. Her fingertip brushed her lip tentatively as if to keep the imprint of his unexpected kiss.

'Luke! Luke Karran!'

The uncertain magic receded. Jenny Qualtrough was calling him from the end of the alley. She was wearing a new dress and bonnet of cherry red that looked striking with her dark hair and brown eyes. Clemence was instantly aware of her own faded gown, but she was prettier than Jenny. It was not immodest to be certain of the fact. Of course, Jenny had the advantage of having a father with his own business. Surely physical attraction was more important than being tied to someone else's money bags? Johanne, she thought desperately, would hate Jenny or any stranger. She was used to the Kinrades.

'I've got to go,' Luke said, removing himself a pace or two. 'But I'll be seeing you, won't I.'

'Don't let me keep you.'

'She'll wait. They always do.'

'But I can't. Goodbye, Luke.' Clemence began to walk very quickly in the opposite direction. She'd not make herself into his door mat however badly she wanted him. Neither did she look back, though the compulsion was overpowering. Let him think he would find it difficult to gain her interest. It would do him good with his wenching and drinking in the

Castletown taverns that ringed the water-front. She'd heard Johanne berating him.

There were ribbons on display at the tiny haberdasher's and she had sufficient money to buy a yellow one as well as the blue she had coveted. It would match the piece of material Jesse had produced the other night. "It's for the Festival", he'd said. "Sorry it was too late for this year. I shouldn't make it up yet. You seem to be shooting up like one of those daffodils in April!"

Remembering Luke's remark about Jesse, Clemence hurried back in case the red-haired girl had returned in her absence. Jesse could be as big a fool as Luke.

But there was no sign of the Irish girl when she returned with the precious package and Clemence's heart lightened. Not even the presence of the female Karrans some yards away could affect her sudden elation. She had always feared Jesse taking up with someone and raggle-taggle Irish riff-raff would be worse than most. Clemence tried to tell herself it was on his behalf that she was concerned, but it was useless to pretend. She did not want to give up the privileged place she had. How honesty could hurt!

All the way home, Fiddler's hide rubbing at her thighs in a fashion more pleasurable than usual and the moon scudding from out of the treetops and back again, she reproached herself for her selfishness. But the cottage had never been so well-tended, and Meg Conroy was for ever telling her that trollops spoiled what decent women cared for. Not that Meg wasn't the best of women, but she had an aversion for dirt and neglect. Bessie and Hugh were always clean as pins. How strange Hugh had been this morning.

The empty sledge scraped lightly against the bumps of the track and Clemence felt free as a bird. Jesse, in spite of his lapses at the market, had the comforting clink of coins in his pocket. The red-haired girl had found some benefactor. They would never see her again. Clemence sang to herself as they skirted the wood.

Jesse went out after their return and a hasty supper

and Clemence, tired but excited in turns, could not sleep once she had gone to her bed in the loft. She heard the Karrans return and slid down the ladder to peer out of the window, the dresser plates dim rounds in the darkness. She saw Johanne and Aggie, hunched in their shawls, go into the house but Luke stood outside, silhouetted against the sky, his broadness tapering to slim shanks in tight breeches.

He must have seen some movement for he began to walk towards the Kinrade cottage. Her heart banged in her chest. The crude glass distorted his features into a mask of darkness tinged with silver.

Luke pushed open the door and stepped inside. She could smell his presence, the sweat and salt and seaweed scent that hung about his clothes.

'Not asleep?' His soft voice mocked her.

'Get out! Get out, do you hear? I'll tell Jesse—'

'You know you won't. Why waste your breath? You've been wanting me to come, haven't you, all these weeks and months.'

He had moved closer and she felt his hand on her wrist. The strong fingers slid up her arm to just above the elbow, then clamped around her breast.

She gasped and tried to free herself but now his other arm was around her body while his fingertips searched through the firm stuff of her nightgown for the hard little nipple.

Clemence pushed at him, not entirely wanting him to release her, yet realising that she was irrevocably lost if he did not.

'Luke! Where are you? Lazy good-for-nothing,' Johanne was grumbling with a soft violence. 'Be the death of him one day, I will.'

'You don't think he's over there?' Aggie suggested, cackling.

'Over where? Kinrades'! That milk-sop? Like a white rat that one is.'

'He must be somewhere.'

'Probably in the spinney with some no-good from Castletown.'

Their voices receded.

'Why didn't you tell 'em I was here?' Luke let go of Clemence so suddenly that she almost lost her balance. 'You could have.'

Ignoring the question, she said, 'Jesse'll be back soon. He won't like finding you in his house. With me.'

'Wasn't really fair to you, Ma wasn't. Jealous she is. More like a bit of a moonbeam, I'd say.' He picked up a strand of her milky hair and let it slide through his fingers. 'See you at the Midsummer junketing, eh? Not much chance round here of getting you to myself. You'll be there, won't you.'

She didn't answer. Couldn't—

'I said, you'll be there, Clemence Kinrade.'

'Yes.'

The stifled whisper seemed to satisfy him. 'Don't you go forgetting, then.' His footsteps grew fainter and died out altogether. It was unreal. It hadn't happened.

She did not know how long she stood there but she became aware that her feet were cold against the bare floor, and, shivering, made her way up the loft stair. Her mind was filled with images of Luke. The square, strong, sensual face half-materialised in the rafters and would not be exorcised. Over and over again she heard Johanne and Aggie denigrating her, then Luke's refutation of their estimate of her. Bit of a moonbeam he'd said. Moonbeams were pretty. Unreal—

Much later, sanity returned. Jesse would never countenance any relationship with Luke Karran. But he need not know. He always went off himself at the Midsummer Festival and she went to Mrs. White's at St. John's, a cousin of Jesse's dead mother. She could tell her they'd made other plans this year. Someone from Peel had offered to take her for a long-delayed visit to Deborah Quine. She'd meet Jesse before he reached Mrs. White's—tell him the old lady had been called away to a sick relation to explain her own early departure from the house. He'd believe that. Mrs. White was kind and conscientious.

Clemence was suddenly sick with self-detestation. Luke would have forgotten all about her promise long before next June. It was nearly a year off. Months anyway.

She closed her eyes but did not shut out the floating counterpart of Luke. Slowly she sank into a shallow sleep into which the darkest dreams began, then crumbled into horror. A face seemed to stare right into her own, then recede.

There were voices in her dream. Little by little she struggled out of the troubled coma.

Jesse was saying, very quietly, 'Just looked at her and the devil himself wouldn't wake her. Always tired out when we get back from market is Clemence.'

'She didn't like me. I could tell.' It was a soft Irish voice, lilting and not unused to pleasing men. Clemence had heard that voice before, on the quay at Castletown.

'Don't suppose she thought any more about you.'

'Oh, but she did. And scowled at me as if I'd been Old Nick himself.'

'Not Clemence.'

'That child's half in love with you.'

'She's my niece.' For the first time, Jesse sounded shocked.

'It's true, though. Know all about men, and women, I do.'

'Hope you know about men,' Jesse said huskily and poked as quietly as he could at the small fire. 'There's brandy there from my last run. Help yourself, Erin Doyle.'

Erin Doyle. The name rang through Clemence's brain like a clarion call. She had forgotten Luke. Luke was not permanent, not like Jesse who so closely resembled her father. How dare Erin Doyle suggest that there was some impropriety in her feelings towards her uncle? How dare she! Meg would sum up the Irish woman in one biting word. Trollop. The word echoed in Clemence's brain, gaining momentum at every moment, one minute soft, the next as loud as a brass trumpet.

The woman was pouring out the brandy. Glasses clinked. They were drinking.

'For God's sake, girl, don't make a noise.'

'You made more stirring the fire.' Erin laughed, a thread of seductive sound.

'We want some bit o' comfort, don't we?' A pink glow had appeared on the wall.

'Course we do, Jesse.'

The hatred that had built up in Clemence reached its apex when the Irish slut said Jesse's name so familiarly. They must have made their plans when she was buying the ribbon and gingerbread at Jesse's suggestion. Bitch! Wide-awake, Clemence listened, her body rigid.

'Oh, come on. You know what I want. What we both want. I'm no skinflint. You don't need to worry that I'll take everything and give nothing. Here,' Jesse was rummaging in the dresser drawer, Clemence recognised its peculiar squeak, 'this is a bit of stuff I got from a wreck—'

'Go on!' Erin was not deceived. 'Smuggled more like.'

'Got to make something extra or life wouldn't be worth living.'

'No. And I'll bet you find it exciting. A fine, strong man like you, wasting yourself on a bit o' land and some fishin'.'

'Sometimes I use it on something else.'

Clemence got off her palliasse and peered through the loft bars. That so familiar squeal of the third dresser drawer. It was *her* material Jesse held in his hands, the piece of pale yellow he'd promised her for the Festival. She could not breathe for the passion that filled her. Erin was fingering it delicately, yet avidly.

''Tis beautiful, Jesse. And for me, you say?'

'For you, my lovely.'

'And what'll you be wanting in return?'

'God, girl. Do I have to say?' Jesse's heavy whisper was filled with a soft thickness that was new and unwelcome. He sounded like Luke with his hand on her breast. The realisation filled Clemence with a pain she did not understand. Without a thought for herself he was squandering her precious material on the dregs of Dublin.

Jesse was taking the shawl from the woman's shoulders and dropping it over a three-legged stool Clemence often used to sit right up to the fire. She'd never use it again.

'Hey,' Erin objected as the brown, spatulate fingers explored the gap at her throat. 'Not so fast. I'd like some more brandy. Have to be in the proper mood, I do.'

Jesse turned away unwillingly to pour another measure while Erin tossed the parcel of yellow stuff on to the table.

'Quiet,' he cautioned and put the glass into the woman's eager hand. 'She won't stir, I know, but there's no use asking for trouble.'

'Well, don't expect me to go lying down outside. I only does it indoors. Hedges is for tinker trash.' The huge, thick-fringed eyes glittered over the edge of the glass and the frail pink glow from the hearth gave the pale skin a spurious life. Jesse gave a groan that was half-pain, half-pleasure.

'Cruel, you are. Forcing a man to wait so long.' He sat down and pulled the woman to his knee. Slowly, he began to undo the buttons on the green bodice.

She should go back to the mattress, Clemence thought, passion replaced by a curious emptiness. But she could not move.

Erin replaced the glass on the edge of the dresser and the firelight sent shivers of orange and rose across the smooth curved side of it, turning it to an object of beauty. Jesse peeled the bodice down to her waist while she detached shapely arms from the narrow sleeves. The tops of her breasts showed above a grubby shift. His head bent towards them, nuzzling greedily. Erin arched her back as the white cotton slid downwards and Jesse thrust himself over her.

'In the mood now, are you?'

'Yes. Oh, yes.' It was the woman who was now breathless and compliant.

'The bed's over there.'

'So I see.' Erin laughed again. And shivered a little as he fumbled with the fastening at her waist. The dress fell in a green puddle close to the fire.

Burn, Clemence thought. Burn so that I may never see you again.

Naked, Erin turned towards the fire-glow to hold out chilled hands. Her white body was more beautiful than the glass bathed with light. The red-gold hair spilled over the indentation of her spine like expensive silk.

Jesse was undressing urgently. Clemence could bear no more. Blindly, she knelt on the palliasse and drew the blanket up to her forehead. Slumped towards the wall, she was aware of the furtive whispers, the creak of Jesse's bed, his soft shushing as Erin giggled a little drunkenly.

'Gone to me head,' the woman explained in a slightly slurred voice. 'Didn't have nothin' to eat all day but a morsel of bread and that sliver of cheese. That froggie little man did offer me a dinner at the hotel by the corner but I couldn't fancy him somehow. Looked as if he'd brass though. That cigar must have cost a bit.'

'More money than most in Castletown has Barney,' Jesse agreed.

'Barney?'

'Kerruish. Builds boats. Has a big house behind Castle Rushen.'

'Saints preserve us! And I refused all that to walk here and never a bite o' supper.'

'Afterwards,' Jesse told her. 'Afterwards you'll have all the supper your stomach will hold. Why did you come if you had better chances? Why? You must have had some reason.'

44

'Because you're a big, strong, good-looking feller and I couldn't help meself.'

Clemence tried to close her ears to the silence, then the soft rustling that became more urgent, the gasping and the queer haunted cry that ended the business.

'For heaven's sake,' Jesse whispered thickly. 'I told you to keep quiet.'

'Ho! You've had what you want and I'm to behave myself. Do I have to take meself off now or can I have the bite you promised?'

'Just keep your voice down and you can have anything you want.' Jesse tiptoed across the floor in the direction of the shelf where the bread and cheese was kept.

'Will she always be up there?' Erin Doyle asked softly. 'Puts me off, she does. I can do better than that if I don't have to restrain meself.'

'Clemence? Where else would she be? This is her home.' Jesse's tone was suddenly curt. 'Look, I shouldn't have said you could have that bit of stuff for a gown. Good as promised it to her, I did.'

'I want it.' Erin's voice sharpened. 'I earned it, didn't I?'

Jesse stood still. There was a long pause, then he said. 'Yes, you did, you red-headed witch. You'd steal a man's heart from his body and laugh as you tossed it away. But I'd not disappoint the child—'

'Not so much of the child! For all her pernickety looks, she's as much a woman as she'll ever be.'

'I'll give you something else—'

'Well, that's sauce for you. Take what you want then back out of your promise! I never comes back to a man who diddles me out o' me dues.'

'Have it then, if it means so much to you. I'll get her a piece even better.'

'Don't let's go casting out over a bit of muslin,' Erin said, suddenly relenting. 'Give that to your niece. I'll wait for mine. I take it ye do want me to come again?'

'You know I do.'

'Aye, I suspected you might.' Again that small,

45

insinuating laugh that made Clemence want to leap at her with extended claws.

'But I don't want—'

'Her to find me here in the morning?' Erin asked shrewdly.

'No. I always kept that side of things apart.'

'There's whole families conceived, born and dragged up in the one room! Why's she so different?'

'Her whole family died in the same night and that leaves scars on a child that don't ever go.'

'Well,' Erin said uncomfortably. 'Put that way—'

'I knew you'd see. There's a little stable next door where Fiddler beds. It's warm and cosy. You'll be fine there.'

'Why didn't you take me in there to begin with? Be a lot freer. Wanted to impress me with that dresser and them fancy dishes, was that it?'

'What if it was?' He was defensive.

'Never been put off by lying in a bit o' straw. What was good enough for Jesus should be good enough for the likes o' meself.'

'That smacks of sacrilege,' Jesse observed but there was amusement in his tone.

'Let's go there now. There's something about this place constrains me. It's—knowing *she's* there, I suppose.'

'You're sure?'

'Course I am. I'll always be straight wi' you, Jesse Kinrade.'

'Straight as a spring!'

Erin stuffed her hand over her mouth to stifle the shrieks that threatened to escape. 'You'll be the death o' me.'

'More like the other way around,' Jesse murmured.

'Now, why should I be the death o' you?' Erin whispered, pulling the shawl over her nakedness while Jesse gathered up her clothes.

'Don't know why I said that. Except that overmuch bedding a woman can be bad for a man, so they say.'

'Then they're wrong. 'Tis an old wives' tale.'

'Let's discover how untrue it is, then.'

Fumbling and giggling, the man and woman let themselves out into the dark. The remnants of the fire collapsed with an unhappy sound.

Clemence, peering down through the narrow slats of wood, saw the parcel of stuff still lying on the table where Erin had so carelessly discarded it. She was dimly aware of descending the ladder at breakneck speed and snatching up the yellow folds, then pushing them into the embers.

'Burn!' she whispered and beat at the bundle with the fire irons. 'Burn. And that harlot with you.'

But all it did was to smoulder and turn black in parts. Defeated, Clemence dropped the fire dogs and collapsed face forward in front of the now cold hearth. The sea had taken Dada and now Erin Doyle had purloined Jesse. But there was still Luke. Luke and Midsummer.

CHAPTER TWO

Jesse closed the door softly, so as not to disturb Clemence. He'd not told her why they sometimes had unexpected treats, yet the child wasn't a fool. But he must never implicate her in his productive little side-line. If she knew nothing, she couldn't blab to Captain Jayce if he ever took it into his head to question her.

The thought of the captain made Jesse grin as he wrapped straw round Fiddler's hooves and fastened the tough, suggane saddle-bags. Softly, he whistled 'The Spanish Lady'. Not that he wanted a Spanish woman. He was very content with Erin Doyle and if he played his cards right she'd become more than his mistress. She was tired of skivvying at the Castle Inn and the clientèle was crude. If he could just show her that there would be falderals as well as life's necessities, Erin could well agree to a more permanent place in his household. Like all women, she wanted pretty things.

There was a light in the Karran shack, a secretive, glimmering reflection as though Johanne sat there making wax dolls and transfixing them with pins. The factor at Ravensdowne always swore she'd overlooked the cows after he'd threatened to take Luke up before his master for poaching. One by one they'd sickened and died and the horse-doctor had found no reason, at least, none that he or anyone else recognised.

Jesse found himself hoping that Clemence was still heeding his wishes and keeping Luke at a proper distance. He'd never once seen them together, though she did walk with Hugh on evenings when her work was finished. She must see how decent and appreciative Meg Conroy's son was and keep a special place for him in her heart. It was time Clemence thought about a future husband and she could do no better.

He whistled quietly all the way through the copse with the moon chasing him between the branches, its bland face the very colour of mistletoe berries.

Once or twice he imagined himself followed and drew Fiddler to a standstill behind a bush but there was only the deep dreaming silence of the dark broken by the faint murmur of water and the swooping flight of an owl.

Reassured, Jesse rode on, more at ease now that he was on the moor and could see for long distances, the track a white wandering scar under the moon. He whistled again, confident now that he'd not be heard, watching the moor diminish in front of him and the familiar scoop of the cliff edge come close.

He tethered the horse to the nearest stone and knelt to light the lantern he had brought. The strike-light was slow to ignite and, as he worked on it, Jesse remembered the day his father had sat in the inn at Castletown with himself and Joseph, and the broad phlegmatic man in seafaring clothes had come to their table. His wide face was a living walnut-shell out of which protruded a long clay pipe. This he had continually sucked as if he could not bear to be parted from it. Jesse, an impressionable eight-year-old, had been fascinated by Captain Ellis from Ravenglass and had later been allowed to see over the captain's boat, *Glass Lady*. She had excited him even more with her dark cabins and towering masts, the high carved prow. The masts had not been as high as Jesse'd imagined, but to a child, they'd seemed to reach into the clouds.

Once he had seen the red sails unfurled and catching the wind, and he'd wanted to stay aboard and sail to Cumberland and beyond, to the world's end.

It was later that Jesse had been initiated into the

monthly ritual of coming here to signal *Glass Lady* and to discover that the stirring and illicit journeys across the rock-strewn bay invariably led to drink, tobacco, silver and tea, the small luxuries that lightened the harsh poverty of their everyday labour.

Not that he should continue to act as Ellis's ferryman once he had a wife and perhaps children dependent on him. No one was infallible—

He stopped trying to light the lantern and froze. Something had moved. The furtive sound set his heart beating and his palms were damp. Always, at the back of his mind, he'd tried to imagine what he'd do under these circumstances but he had no more than his fists and his wits to help him escape.

Fiddler moved restlessly and Jesse's ears burned. The long moments passed. There was only the sound of the sea below and a susurration of breeze in the heather. Surely an exciseman would have challenged him by now? Jesse, crouched low, watched the slight swell of the ground from which the small noise had proceeded. And then, his breath was expelled on a great gasp that turned to a snort of laughter. Against the sky appeared the silent shape of a large cat. It bounded away at the sudden uproar and Jesse had to press his fist against his mouth. This time it was a harmless encounter with a roving tom. If he wasn't quiet it could be a confrontation of a very different calibre.

The shock had taken some of his strength and his wrist shook as he lit the lantern and held it towards the sea, passing his other hand three times across the horn pane. The moon had gone behind the clouds and the sea was a dark gulf below the cliff.

The answering light came suddenly, swinging against a horizon as nebulous as the sea. Unsteadily, Jesse unfastened the straps of the straw panniers and tied them to his back. He doused the lantern and lowered himself onto the beginning of the steep, stony track to the little bay. Usually his nerve was good and he travelled quickly down the distorted gradient with its unexpected drops and loose rock. Tonight, he fumbled and hesitated, cursing himself for his stupidity. When the moonlight returned, he made the mistake of looking down at the most perilous point of the descent. That moment of idiocy with his hands still damp from his earlier fright and his equilibrium gone, was a mistake.

His feet slid on a loosened stone and for a moment he hung spread-eagled, his fingers slipping from their insecure handhold and one foot seeking frantically for some ledge or crevice to take his endangered weight. The stone bounced from ledge to ledge and cracked spitefully against boulders below.

Jesse's toe slid into a crevice and lodged there. He laid his face against the cold rock, his chest heaving painfully. The path had never had unknown terrors before tonight. Was he getting too old for the exercise?

He waited until his breathing was less uneven, then willed himself to go on. It was usually so easy! Now, because an over-sexed tom had decided to travel to a neighbouring barn, he had crumbled. Jesse despised himself.

His foot crunched on the shingle. It seemed that aeons had passed but the descent could have taken only a few minutes. His natural optimism asserted itself and he even whistled as he pushed the little boat down the hand-made slipway and slung his leg over the side. A few undulations and he had his balance. His arms rowed strongly towards the dim bulk of *Glass Lady*, now just visible in the gun-metal mass of sky and sea, but all the time his ears were cocked for any sign of the unusual. The brush with death or injury had left its mark. He didn't intend to die now that Erin had come into his life, wanting him as he needed her.

The great wall of the vessel reared up before him and a rope snaked out of nowhere. Jesse tied the boat and went up, hand over hand. Ellis and the first mate, Jones, were waiting, pistols in evidence, in case Jesse was not their expected midnight visitor.

It was warm in the cabin and fuggy with the fumes

51

of Ellis's pipe, but the rum was good, putting fresh vigour into Jesse. Again, he was deeply ashamed at his earlier faint-heartedness. Perhaps falling in love with a woman altered a man's viewpoint, made him appreciate his own skin as a single person would not. But he still could not forgive his own girlishness at the only intimidating point on the declivity.

Ellis's voice rumbled on, a comforting drone. Jones packed the panniers and the captain brought out a parcel and a bundle of lace. 'For your sweetheart,' he told Jesse with the lop-sided leer that passed for a smile. 'What's she like this time?' He always joked about Jesse's faithlessness. 'Is't still Molly?'

'No. This one's an Irish lass. Red-haired—'

'Be a handful, then, in more ways than one,' Captain Ellis pronounced, the pipe dragging down the left-hand side of his mouth even further. 'Watch out for red hair. There'll be tantrums. Broken crocks—'

'Plenty of those,' Jesse agreed, opening the parcel. A shimmer of green silk slid onto the lamplit table. His heart leapt. Erin wouldn't be able to resist this. She was mad for the colour. His fingers ran along the fine softness as though it were her skin he touched. 'Aye,' he said, trying not to appear too enthusiastic, 'it'll do. But next time I want all silver. I—I need the money.'

He stuffed the lace into a capacious pocket and re-wrapped the bolt of silk.

'I'll be two hours,' he told Ellis and now all trace of insufficiency had gone.

'No more,' Ellis replied.

'No more.'

He was shinning down the rope and the moon was out again and smiling down at him enigmatically. Jesse was no longer thinking of the rides to the big coastal houses and the furtive deliveries. He was thinking of Erin in a green gown with lace round neck and cuffs. A grateful Erin who'd forget she'd had to take that sleazy job in the inn to keep body and soul together while she debated her future.

Whistling, he cast off and started for the shore.

* * *

He was to marry Erin. Clemence had not believed it at first. After all Jesse knew of that woman's past! But it was the present that had ensnared him, those supposedly secret visits to the stable with the door shut against the weather. Then he had brought the Irishwoman to supper with himself and Clemence.

Erin was attired in a new green gown, the material certainly supplied by Jesse. Clemence had one also. Jesse had found the spoiled remains of the yellow muslin in the hearth and imagined them destroyed accidentally because of Erin's carelessness.

Clemence was silent throughout the meal, but Erin more than made up for that in frenetic chatter until even her subtle invention gave out.

'Have you nothing to say?' Jesse demanded, exasperated.

'No.'

'Not even when Erin is to be your new aunt?' Jesse brought her back to the present.

'Don't force the child. It's a lot to get used to.'

'There'll be less work for you to do,' Jesse mumbled.

'There'll be nothing for me to do.'

'You'll be getting wed yourself,' Erin suggested slyly.

Clemence, aware of a growing lump in her throat, got up and ran from the room. But there was no comfort in either the wood or later at the Conroys who knew all about Jesse's obsession with Erin Doyle. All Meg's cleanliness, and good wholesome looks, the sun-kissed freckles, could not dim the spectre of Erin as mistress at Kinrades'.

''Tis true then,' Meg said, seeing Clemence's tight pallor when she mentioned the supper-party.

'They'll wed as soon as the new room's finished.'

'I saw Jesse had started it. He'll have it ready in a month or so,' Bessie ventured.

'It had to happen,' Meg said kindly. 'A man needs a

53

wife, lass. Maybe she'll keep him from such daftness as flouting the law. He's no longer a lad needing to find his excitement in contraband.'

'She likes him to bring home things. It puts her in a good mood and that's what Jesse enjoys above everything else!'

'You mustn't be so bitter. You wouldn't like it if the boot was on the other foot and they turned against you for wanting a lad of your own.'

Though she had not specified Hugh, Clemence was perfectly well aware that Meg's ambition was the same as Jesse's. A pity they would both be disappointed.

'You don't want to stay a maid all your life, do you?' Meg went on, offering Clemence a cup of tea. The tea had been a gift from Jesse and was only brought out on special occasions. Clemence's present unhappiness was one of those, Meg had decided generously.

'Of course not.' Clemence's mind was immediately filled with pictures of Luke. She remembered the pressure of his mouth, his hand on her body, the way he smiled.

'Well, then,' Meg said with one of her indulgent looks. 'Drink your tea, love.'

She'd been very good to her, Clemence acknowledged, the edge taken off her misery. But why couldn't Jesse have married someone warm and comfortable? Someone she could have liked?

The fire was burning in the spotless grate, beautifying the cosy room that was such a part of her growing up. Here she had learnt to spin and weave, to make ropes and to wash clothes. She had even helped Meg and dear, plain, kind Bessie to drag pebbles from Kitterland Sound to make borders for the Conroy flower beds.

Clemence drew closer to the warm murmur of the fire, like a starved cat. Every time she had a bad thought about Erin, she'd replace it with another about Luke, a Luke grown different, more constant and who'd never go off with the Jenny Qualtroughs of the world.

54

'You'll get a new gown, anyway, if there's to be a wedding,' Bessie told her, pulling a stool up to the hearth. 'Jesse won't see you go without.' Her well-scrubbed face showed nothing but the simple goodness that was her essence.

'He's a fine man,' Meg agreed, sipping her own tea, 'and deserves a bit of happiness. When you've gone, the place would have been lonely for him.'

'I'd never have gone away!'

'Oh?' Meg said softly. 'Then you'd pick someone close at hand?'

'Perhaps.'

'Would it be—?' Bessie began excitedly, but her mother slapped her on the knee.

'Don't ask what should be private. Clemence'll tell us in her own good time. Maybe she hasn't been asked. Yet.'

'What's this?' Hugh demanded, darkening the doorway and looking even older than when Clemence had last seen him. His teeth were very white and shiny. Meg always made her family use salt and soot to clean them and Clemence had adopted the habit. It was certainly effective.

'Jesse's getting wed,' Meg said swiftly, rising to give Hugh a mug of the precious tea.

'To the girl from the Castle Inn. She's a Dubliner,' Bessie supplemented, passing her brother an oatcake.

She's a whore, Clemence thought stonily, the familiar sense of belonging spoiled and meaningless. She had felt like this only once or twice before. The night of the Clay Head storm and the evening Jesse had introduced Erin to his home. Think of the future, she told herself desperately. Think of a life with Luke. Being everything to him. It was shameless how much she wanted him. She was alarmed and yet excited by the fever in her blood.

'I'll come with you,' Hugh said as she rose to go.

'There's no need—'

'But I'd like to. There's still some daylight. We can walk through the copse.'

Clemence would much rather have walked alone with her clamouring urges and daring thoughts, but, like coming here for comfort and advice, it was customary to be accompanied by Hugh who had been like a brother until that episode on market day. Now she was forced to admit there was no longer anything fraternal in his feelings and regretted the loss of the bond that once existed.

She kept a distance between them as they walked along the wide track, the light filtered through the changing leaves. It was some time before she noticed Hugh's unaccustomed silence, so engrossed was she in her own private imaginings. She must still answer to Jesse for her behaviour at supper! Her feelings swung on a pendulum of irritation towards Jesse and detestation of Erin.

It was when the path narrowed that she and Hugh were suddenly close together. She quickened her pace.

'Clemence,' Hugh said in the stifled fashion she had learnt to recognise in other men. Alarm signals sounded in her blood. 'Don't run away from me.'

'I must go home. I've been out too long.'

He lengthened his stride and caught up with her quite easily. His fingers were strong around her delicate wrist. Staring up at him, she saw that his eyes were dark with an animation that had the effect of arousing guilt. He shouldn't have put her in the position of having to hurt him so badly.

She attempted to escape by pulling against his locked fingers but he wouldn't let go of her hand.

'You must know what I'm going to say—'

'Don't say anything—'

'I must. I can see you may not be ready to listen but I have to tell you that I'm much in love with you, Clemence—'

'You can't be!' she cried. 'You mustn't be. Please, Hugh.'

'Is it so terrible to be told that a man loves you?'

'It is, when—'

'When what?' His brows were drawn into a frown

and the usually pleasant mouth was thinned into a line. 'What are you afraid of?'

'I can't love you.'

'Maybe you don't at the moment but I want you to think of what I've said. Then, later, perhaps—'

'But there won't be any later and I don't want you to waste your time on me. Don't you understand? I won't ever want you for a husband! That's only Jesse and your mother and wishful thinking. I—can't.'

'You only think so now. I should have waited. I realise that. But I was afraid you'd never see what was under your nose.'

'I knew all right, that day you picked me out of the ditch. But it hasn't made me want to come closer to you and it would have if I felt loving towards you.'

Hugh released her and the feeling rushed painfully into her wrist. She rubbed at it and he said, 'I'm sorry. I didn't mean—'

'It's nothing. Do go back, now. Please—'

'Is my company so distasteful to you?'

'Don't be hurt! It's not your fault. It's nobody's fault. How could it be?'

'But you won't forget altogether, will you? I'm not going to change. If you should need me, Clemence, you only have to let me know.'

'Very well. But don't hope for too much, Hugh. I must be honest.'

He bowed his head and his features were blurred in the encroaching dimness. 'The only thing I have left is hope. Don't take that away.'

'You haven't listened!'

'Oh, but I have. I just think you may not really know your own mind yet.'

'But the rest of you do! Oh, good night, Hugh.' It was useless to warn him.

Still he hesitated, then he said, 'Good night, my dear.'

She listened to his receding footsteps, remembering the unexpected tenderness of those last words. Clemence, drained of energy by the recent battle of wills, remained leaning against a slender birch trunk, her arms by her sides. Nothing of what Hugh had said really surprised her.

She stayed where she was, unwilling to return to Jesse's cottage, a little tired and wishing only for a peace she had begun to realise was not for her. Then there were arms around her waist, locking her fast to the birch stem. Clemence tore at the strong interlaced fingers.

* * *

Luke had heard everything. Earlier he had noticed Clemence running out of the Kinrade cottage, her hair and her dress floating. It was always this suggestion of someone other-worldly that fascinated him. The shape of the girl through diaphanous layers of summer clothing and her dazzling fairness had always wrought strongly upon his imagination. The way her eyes widened and became a jewel-blue when he came upon her in solitude. The little veins in her eyelids and the shadows of her eye-sockets that were palest lavender. Her small, narrow bones.

Mixed with the desire to force himself upon her was a compulsion to squeeze her white flesh until she cried out in pain and bruises stood out on her body.

He had followed her. She had not known because he had a gipsy-like skill at tracking. The sight of her skirt billowing in the breeze as she sped between the trees worked on his senses like an aphrodisiac. She was like a butterfly or a flower.

Luke derided himself for the unaccustomed flight of fancy. Down in Castletown he regularly experienced the physical satisfaction one derived from ordinary women but Clemence Kinrade was outside this normal intercourse. From the first moment he'd set eyes on her as a grief-stricken child he had considered her his own possession, to be claimed when the moment was right. And now Hugh had put that intention in jeopardy by declaring his own ridiculous passion and demanding that Clemence learn to think of him as a future husband.

For a moment Luke envisaged the pair locked in the intimacy of marriage and found that he could not endure the notion. He had been forced to clench his fists and remain in hiding when all his impulses cried out for him to spring out on Conroy and beat the life out of him. If Clemence had wavered in her determination—

But she had not. She had sent Conroy away because of himself and saved that young prig from maiming or worse.

For a time Luke contented himself with watching her against the tree. Her eyes had closed and her lips parted. Hunger grew in him, yet it was mixed with caution. She would expect permanence and there was Jenny to be considered. She had told him that the shop would come to her on her father's death and the old man was not in good health. Almost as strong as Luke's need for Clemence was the compulsion to become master of that tidy little business and the neat, small house that went with it. Why couldn't Clemence have owned a shop in the town? Qualtrough's. He'd never have that chance again. He mustn't throw it away.

The thought of Jenny Qualtrough and the shop faded as he concentrated on Clemence's unaware and ethereal figure. Farm girls were apt to be stocky and none too fastidious but Meg had instilled her own need for cleanliness into the girl so that she always gave out her own, unspoiled attraction as a flower enticed bees. Taking her would be like tearing a honeysuckle bloom or killing a moth. Clemence had never been entirely flesh and blood. He did not know if he wanted her to be.

She sighed as though she were preparing to go and he moved swiftly and silently until he was behind the sapling, then wound his arms around tree and girl as if they were one.

The feel of the soft indentation of her waist excited

59

him. There was no Jenny, no town, no village, only Clemence pinioned and struggling. A butterfly on a pin—

He did not understand his own destructive urges. He only knew that they were dark and deep and compelling and that he must indulge them.

'It's me, Clemence. You knew it was, didn't you?' He pulled her round to face him, for once unable to laugh at the mingling of fear and sensuousness in her gaze. A blurred finger of moonlight touched her and all at once he was kissing her violently, tearing at her bodice and letting his lips travel downwards into the hollow between her small breasts. She shivered and was still.

She did not push him away immediately and he entertained a wild hope that she meant to allow him to possess her, but when he began to fumble at the barrier of clothes between them, she jerked herself free.

'I want you,' he said.

'I—I know.'

'I mean to have you and I want it to be now.' He tried to calm the quickening of his breath but still the words tumbled over one another.

'Oh, Luke—' Her hand fluttered towards him. It had grown still darker and she was a phantom beckoning.

He took the soft whisper for assent and returned to the business of seduction but again she was afraid, holding him off with more strength than her appearance of fragility warranted. 'Not like this—' she pleaded.

Angrily, he let her go. She fell to her knees. Even the unexpected movement was graceful and he almost hated her as she stared up at him beseechingly.

'Don't think you'll make me promise anything I don't want!' he shouted.

Her moonlit face was curiously empty as though he had destroyed what lay behind it. 'I'm tired, Luke. There's nothing I want now.'

'And it doesn't matter how I feel?'

'I didn't say that.'

'Well, if you expect me to offer what *he* did, you're mistaken.'

'He?' She frowned. 'He? You mean—Hugh?'

'Who else should I mean!'

'How dare you spy—'

'You're growing too big for your boots, Miss Kinrade. Just because I want a tumble, you build it into a drama. Girls are ten a penny—'

'Some,' she said cuttingly. 'I'm not like Jenny Qualtrough, hanging around the Castletown back streets just in case your shadow happens to fall over hers. I don't want to be any man's whore.' All the bitterness of her feelings towards Erin was in the declaration, but Luke didn't know that.

'Then we have nothing more to discuss.' He pushed at her kneeling figure as he passed and felt her hand grasp at his ankle. To hell with her he thought, furious and frustrated. He could have forced her but they were too near Croggan and the memory of Jenny and all that came with her was filtering back into his consciousness.

He kicked Clemence's hand away and left her without another look. But before he reached his own door he acknowledged that the rape of Jesse's niece was not what he wanted. The real pleasure would be in having Clemence pleading for him to lie with her. There was still one little corner in his savage nature that did not enjoy destroying butterflies.

* * *

It was not only the green silk that had induced Erin to accept Jesse's offer of wedlock. He'd made the offer weeks back when she told him, rather pale-faced and hesitant, that she was pregnant, which was no thunder-clap to either considering the violence of their mutual passion, though he was surprised that she was so large after only three months.

'It's going to be a big child,' Erin had said, pressing his hands to her belly. 'You're no midget, are you.'

'I never thought it showed much before four or five months.'

'You know nothing,' Erin had said, smiling in her devastating fashion. 'You're such an innocent in some respects.'

He was amazed at the way he regretted her own sophistication, and she, reading the anger in his eyes, said, 'It's not every woman would give up the likes of that Barney Kerruish for a tenant smallholder. Now, is it!'

'No.'

'He still looks at me on market days as though he'd eat me alive. A little frog who'll never turn into a fairy prince, whatever the old tales say.'

It was as much the implied threat of Kerruish as the knowledge of her condition that had made him suggest marriage, a state he'd evaded for over thirty years without the slightest compunction.

But Jesse extracted Erin's promise that they'd wait a little so that Clemence would grow used to the idea. After all, that would rob them of nothing they hadn't already enjoyed. And the bedroom would take time.

Jesse would not easily forget his hasty marriage. Erin wore the green gown he liked most, and new green stockings and garters. The silver-buckled shoes were his own gift, as was the shawl of loaghtyn wool and the cloak against the wintry weather. He'd taken her back to Croggan on the sledge, covered with a loaghtyn rug, she laughing at the fine curtain of snowflakes that came on in the afternoon, settling like lace on the darkened countryside.

He stopped to embrace her and she clung to him, exulting in her new state. 'I do love you, Jesse.'

'And I love you, lass. But why did you choose the green for a wedding-gown? I've given you other colours.'

'You're not superstitious, are you? I thought you as ungodly as meself.'

'I am, and yet—'

But she kissed away his doubts and he wanted her then and there only she pushed him away, reminding him that she wasn't gipsy trash to be taken under a hedge. 'There's our beautiful new bedroom, Jess Kinrade, and I'm six months gone—'

'Five, surely?'

'Sure, and me head's so turned with the switches and changes, I don't remember. But you will be right, love. I'm a simple girl as you must know. Bad at figuring. And anyway, what does it matter? What's time, after all?'

'What, indeed?' Jesse agreed, his heart thudding at the feel of her under the cloak. Yet it did matter. He'd not forgotten he wasn't the first man in her life. He pushed back the doubts as she had smilingly repulsed his advances, remembering how Erin would respond in the private bedroom he had built. There was only the matter of Clemence to resolve.

When they reached home it was as bad as he'd feared. Clemence was in the living-room, ghost-like and unforgiving. He'd not been able to bring himself to tell her this was the day. All the bowel-gripping excitement of the occasion and the gradually snow-bound return was dissipated by her white-faced repudiation of the fact that Erin was now his wife for better or worse.

But there was no time for Clemence to say what she thought for Jesse had taken the precaution of inviting all his neighbours from miles around, including the Karrans. It would have been bad luck not to ask Johanne and her insolent brood. No man would fancy a pin stuck in his waxen effigy on his wedding-night. Johanne could have made him impotent. She'd done it before to the factor's son because of that business of Luke and his poaching. It was not only the cows that had withered and died.

But he mustn't laugh! Marriage was too serious for that. Tonight he must thole the Karran family. No one would think less of him for it.

The Conroys appeared almost immediately, carrying the bulk of the food that had been secreted with Meg until it was needed. Brand and his son and daughter-in-law had arrived from Ravensdowne and old Jem Walsh from Four Corners, with his family. Dick Roberts from Windstraw with Emily. Peter Qualtrough and Donald Christian with their wives, from Port St. Mary. Some of the guests Clemence did not recognise.

The Kinrade cottage was quickly filled from end to end and the sound of the fiddle stole out among the trees and mossy copses, disturbing the owls and night creatures. The snow had stopped and was thin enough to be beautiful but to be no real deterrent to visitors. Peats were stacked high on the fire and the floorboards shook. Croggan was alive and tingling with expectation.

Hugh had captured Clemence early and she could not show him her white despair at Jesse's so conclusive action. All these months she had buoyed herself with the thought that he could quite easily have cold feet when the time approached, but Erin's altering figure was a warning even she could not ignore.

Meg had made light of it. Country folk often contracted marriages in this fashion and Clemence would surely not expect Jesse to act dishonourably? What if the boot was on the other foot and some other man had overcome Clemence's scruples?

'I wouldn't do that! Not ever.'

'I'm glad, lass. I'm no decrier of principles. I'd like to think Hugh's wife—'

There was no need to finish the sentence. Hugh's wife must be a paragon and Clemence was conscious only of her own lack of suitable qualities. She was the sort who'd prefer trash like Luke. Luke—

Jesse, watching her uneasily, was eventually deceived by Clemence's pale calmness. She was coming round: realising that nothing could be changed. His eyes searched the room for his new wife and saw her dancing with Brand's son. She would cure his impotence if anyone could. Erin was capable of arousing any man. The green silk, the lace and the cascade of red hair spun and twisted, outlined in fire-glow and candleshine. Suddenly he wished the evening was over and done with. It didn't matter that he'd already had her. Tonight was new and precious. A beginning—

Bessie was dancing with Brand, her plain, buxom wholesomeness a painful contrast to Clemence's floating unsubstantiality. She made everyone else look earthy and over-solid. Meg pranced with her erstwhile quiet Jim, emboldened by ale and a tot of rum, her white teeth flashing. All the Conroys had splendid teeth.

The end of a particularly exuberant jig coincided with the entry of the Karrans, Johanne tall and majestic in a dark, sack-like robe of indeterminate origin, her black eyes flashing. A hush fell over the heated conclave. Brand, senior and junior, changed colour and retreated into the shadows. Silence engulfed the room.

Aggie had her wild hair tamed into incredible submission. She was a thin-faced version of Luke who was, in the candleglow and rushlight, as splendid as a prince from the Orient. Someone coughed and the spell was broken.

Jesse had a sudden, disconcerting glimpse of Clemence clothed in white fire, her eyes like precious stones. Staring— But his mind shied away from the possibility of any entanglement. She wouldn't be so heedless and foolish. The child was patently afraid of Johanne, intimidated by Aggie's crazy laughter. Perhaps they'd go soon.

Erin claimed him, her fingers curiously predatory as if she had ceased to be the girl he knew the instant the ring was on her hand. But he did not care who she was. The touch of her beautiful, fecund body aroused all of the old excitement. The emerald gown covered her like a soft skin and there was a scent of herbs in her hair. He'd never let her go.

Someone had followed Luke into the noisy room but Clemence did not see her immediately. It was not until the Roberts joined the dance that she recognised the tall dark girl with the air of authority. It was Jenny. Jenny with her hand laid possessively on Luke's fore-arm, smiling up into his absorbed face. They shut out everyone else. How dare he invite her!

Clemence felt physically ill. First the shock of Jesse wedding, almost in secret, then the Qualtrough girl flaunting her relationship with Luke. Jenny with her expectations and a good body to go with them. Even Clemence had to admit the fact.

Surely Luke hadn't meant all the things he'd said before they parted in the copse? She had expected a period of coldness but not this ostracism. Although Luke's eyes had passed over her more than once they had contained nothing but an impersonal rejection she could not bear. It was as if she had ceased to exist. Limbo hurt.

The dance ended, Luke left Jenny near the hearth, chatting to the Brands who were customers at her father's shop. He strode across the room and Clemence thought he meant to approach her at last. Cruelly, he allowed her to accost him with a tentative 'Hello, Luke. I didn't know you were coming. Is—is all well with us again? Say that it is. I hate us to be estranged—'

He stared straight through her and continued towards the table where the food was laid out. He put some of the unaccustomed delicacies onto a plate which he took to a bridling Jenny.

I hate him, Clemence thought, the bitterness of the entire day accentuated into a black load that lay over her heart, constricting and merciless. But it wasn't true. She might *want* to hate him but that was a different matter.

Johanne was not pleased by the sight of Luke and Jenny. Jesse was not the only one to notice the way her dark, snake-like eyes continually sought out the couple, and the increasing discomfort of Miss Qualtrough who could not possibly remain unaware of Johanne's visible enmity. That silent hostility could shake the staunchest resolve. It seemed that any ideas Luke might have for an early announcement would be severely curtailed. In any case, those who knew old Qualtrough were certain that he'd never give his consent to any engagement to the likes of a Karran, and though failing, he still could linger for years. But the presence of Jenny had added a fillip to the celebration. Erin was by now a familiar figure and there was little unusual about the legitimising of a stable relationship. The men all wished—or nearly all—that they were in Jesse's place, for his new wife was striking and obviously bedworthy. The women all had a twinge of sympathy for Clemence whose nose was so indubitably out of place. She'd not have her troubles to seek.

Hugh, realising Clemence's heartache, though not Luke's part in it, was the essence of kindness, fetching her ale and titbits from the unaccustomedly laden table, talking to the girl of everything and nothing, telling himself that when she'd adjusted, she might see that her own home could be what she needed. If only she were not so far away, more comfortable to be with, less complicated. But she was so lovely in her own queer fashion, more dream than reality.

Jesse, seeing that the party was going well enough for him to disappear for a short time with Erin without comment, signalled to his bride. She was not over large with the child, just slightly rounded and more womanly. Not that that had made Erin Doyle any less desirable in Jesse's eyes. Erin Kinrade. His pulse beat the faster, visualising the night ahead. He'd limewashed the new room and carved a bed that would last longer than they did. There was a straw mat on the floor to shut out the cold. A sheepskin on the bed. Pillows with dried lavender. A candle to show him the beauty of her hair. A steel mirror to show her the loveliness of her face. As if she did not already know!

Later, when he and his bride were snugly beneath the sheepskin rug and the fever in his blood temporarily assuaged, he asked in a voice changed with passion, 'Are you happy, my darling?'

'Aye,' she replied lazily, 'though I'd like fine a couple o' new gowns—'

'But you've just had one!'

'Did you forget that your bairn's making me increase?'

'A kirtle then and a thick jersey to keep out the cold. You can let out a kirtle and a jersey stretches.'

'My, but you're sounding like a skinflint already, crooch mochree!'

'I'll try, Erin, but the weather won't allow for smuggling. In a month or two—'

'And a gold ring with a green stone like a cat's eye? Please?'

'Erin—'

Her hand passed over his thigh and his crotch, seemingly careless.

'I will. I promise.' His breathing quickened.

'Soon?'

'Soon.' And be damned to Jayce and his informants!

The hand travelled over his chest and moved to his shoulder and the space between his shoulder blades.

His mouth fastened on her throat and the hollow beneath it.

They did not speak again for a time. There was no need. Eventually Jesse stirred lazily and said, 'It's time we went back again, love.'

'With all that racket, they must be enjoying themselves well enough without us.'

'I know. But we're the hosts. And they've been open-handed with wedding gifts, food and the like.'

'Yes, I s'pose so.' Erin yawned and showed most of her pretty, cat-like teeth. The curve of her shoulder in the greenish rushlight almost made Jesse forget his manners and stay where he was. But the splendour of the new chamber could not entirely outweigh the delights of the stable and the benevolent glow of the horn lantern. The future stretched ahead like a long, golden road to perpetual bliss. This was their sanctum.

Unwillingly, they dressed, and as slowly returned to their guests who, obviously, had not really missed them. Erin thanked Johanne for her present of eggs while mentally deciding she'd never eat one of them herself. Clemence would reap the benefit, if she could find the silly, jealous young chit.

Perhaps she was outside with Hugh? But he was there with Meg and Bessie, and Luke Karran was distinctly Jenny Qualtrough's property. The girl's thin, vivacious face was filled with something Erin understood. Iron determination to surmount any obstacle that presented itself. She'd be prepared to wait until old Bob Qualtrough died, as he inevitably must, and face up to Johanne into the bargain. Luke's mother would come to accept that a successful man's money could oil the wheels of her old age as nothing else would. Two or three years and it would all be resolved.

Jesse noted Clemence's disappearance with a chill of pre-knowledge. For all his bravado he knew the depths of the girl's misery. They'd lived so closely over the years that any change in her was immediately visible. She'd never taken to Erin and now that he'd regularised the union she deplored, she'd been mortally wounded. She'd be out in her precious woods, probably, communing with the moon and water. Clemence had always been a misfit. Never a real country girl. Never anything an ordinary man could understand. He hated to hurt her, but neither could he give up a woman he loved for her childish whim. That was his niece's main trouble. She'd never grown up. Something in her make-up had been arrested that terrible night Joseph, Lily and Sammy had died. Clemence was a callow girl struggling against the inevitable erosion of adolescence and womanhood, but with the weapon of being able to touch one to the quick, without the least effort.

He fended off the jocular observations of Donald Christian who had not been unaware of the bridegroom's temporary disappearance, and sought out Erin who was with Dinah Roberts. 'I can't find Clemence.'

'She can't be far,' Erin said. 'She's probably pouring out her troubles to Fiddler. I hope she'll not be —difficult. I wish you'd show her who's master, Jesse?'

Jesse could not blame his wife for expressing her doubts. Clemence had never troubled to disguise her dislike of Erin. It might have been better if the girl had gone to Deborah Quine's at Peel in the first place. And yet—

'She mustn't be allowed to hurt you,' Jesse insisted without too much conviction. His Erin could take care of herself. He was the one in the unhappy position of being pig in the middle.

There was a lull in the festivities as everyone clustered around Roberts who was insisting upon hammering his gift of a horseshoe above Jesse's door.

'He'll end up fixing his hand there instead,' Jim Conroy warned, 'the amount of ale he's drunk.'

'Perhaps we'd best go,' Roberts's wife said, looking out at the thin covering of snow. A solitary set of small footprints led away from the cottage in the direction of the copse.

Jesse, seeing them, was conscious of a swift panic. The only person unaccounted for was Clemence and the snow would not lie for long.

'The stupid little cat,' Erin breathed at his side. 'She's not in the stable, then.'

'I must go and look for her.'

'On our wedding-night!' Erin sounded outraged.

'You didn't expect me just to go back to bed as if nothing had happened!' He flung off her restraining hand.

'No—'

'I couldn't, Erin. I'm responsible for her.'

The waves of fresh air, chilled with the touch of snow, were sobering the gay company. Hugh was at the door, his expression touched with foreboding.

'We'll all look for the girl,' Roberts was insisting, the horseshoe forgotten. The Brands were already putting on their coats while the women living nearby were

70

preparing to go home. Johanne was already halfway to her ramshackle dwelling, her tall figure straight as a rail, leaving the customary aura of disquiet in her wake.

All the activity was blotting out the pathetic trail Clemence had left but Jesse knew its progress by heart. The only thing that might hinder him was the lack of snow in the more sheltered places. It could be difficult to trail her far beyond the entrance to the wood.

He fetched Fiddler and set off, all too aware of Erin's repressed anger.

* * *

Clemence walked through the familiar terrain like an automaton. She had felt the cold at first, but after a time that had worn off, leaving her almost without any bodily sensation and even the black despair numbed.She could not see where her future led.

There had been a pain in her chest this last week but even that had diminished to a nagging irritation in her side.

She had not consciously thought at first of any permanent departure, but minute by minute, the pain of Luke's unmistakable rejection had grown into an uncontrollable monster that menaced her entire being. He was the only person, other than Jesse, to win her total love.

Friendship was sweet, but it was not sufficient.

She knew now that Hugh would not be averse to marrying her but Clemence wanted more than an alliance based merely on friendship. She wanted what Joseph and Lily had had and what Jesse and Erin enjoyed. It was Luke she needed to supply the magic in her life, only he seemed not to care and she thought her heart would break. Yet for all her sickness of heart she still could see his dark side and recognised the fact that he was unlikely ever to make her happy. How ill she felt suddenly and yet she had to keep going somewhere.

71

Deciding that she could not return home, Clemence began to walk through the wood. Moonlight fell bleakly through gaps on to tangled roots and long dead leaves. She trudged out of the trees almost blindly, unaware that she followed the old track by instinct. The heather and dwarf gorse lay on either side, clutching at her ankles through the thick kirtle. She had lost all sense of time.

The sky had grown to an immensity of scudding cloud and the ground was sloping ahead towards the sullen gleam of the sea. She wished she had fallen into the waves with Mama and Sammy. They would all have been with Joseph where they belonged.

To the left of the slope lay the Chasms. Clemence had been warned against them regularly by an anxious Jesse. 'Death traps they are,' he reiterated. 'Never be deceived by them, lass. You step onto heather only there's no rock beneath it, only gaps with a thin cover over them, shafts that can pitch you down near as far as the sea. Two hundred feet leaves no body unbroken, Clemence! Are you listening? There's no second chance.'

She had listened, shuddering, to his tales of the death traps and they had walked over to view them from a safe distance, then taken the cliff-top path towards Spanish Head by Bay Stacka. The Sugar Loaf had loomed out of the water, dark and inimical as Johanne Karran's eyes.

Clemence was impaled on a lance of purest pain. She was trembling violently and it appeared that she had been for some time, but the condition had only just registered. Her breath caught on another stab of agony. It was as though her lung had been pierced. She'd been breathless for several days but had pushed the knowledge from her mind because of the rebellion against Jesse. How could she live in the same house as that whore from Ireland? But perhaps she would not need to. Surely she was dying?

Gasping and clutching at her side, Clemence sank down on to the springy heather and closed her eyes, then began crawling, infinitely slowly, towards the Chasms.

* * *

It was dawn when Jesse found her. After her footprints had been lost he had searched most of the night in all the copses and folds of the country around Croggan, then, in daylight, had saddled Fiddler and ridden further afield. Recognising the girl's unhappiness, he'd eventually thought of the cliffs that represented escape from life's problems. She had always been fascinated and repelled by the heights that led to Spanish Head and the invisible threat of the Chasms. If only Clemence could bring herself to accept his wife. He couldn't gainsay Erin. If she asked him to throw himself off the highest cliff in Man, he'd do it, such was her power over his senses.

But he loved Clemence in his fashion as he realised only too clearly, kneeling beside the frail, deathlike body. He'd have been a fool not to sense her previous affection and her present despair. None of this would have happened had she accepted Deborah's invitation to go with her as her charge. Perhaps when Clemence was better, it could be suggested that she have a holiday at Peel. He could take her over himself with Fiddler's help and the sledge and explain his new circumstances to Mistress Quine. No such problems would arise in that quarter and Clemence required stability.

And Erin needed the house to herself for a bit. He exulted in the thought even as he smoothed the ashen hair from the child's forehead and felt for her heartbeat. Perhaps Erin was right, after all, about Clemence's maturity. Her breast was well-formed if a trifle inadequate. He liked a woman to be large in the proper places.

Concern overcame everything else as he took the still body before him on the waiting horse. The child's colour was bad and she'd obviously lain there for hours, just on the fringe of the Chasms. Thank God her strength had given out before she'd crawled far enough.

The surgeon pronounced inflammation of the lungs and advised prolonged rest and nursing.

As he had expected, Erin was none too pleased to be expected to act as nursemaid and she six months gone.

'Six?'

'Five, I mean, of course! It was the sight of her made me forget meself. But I'm feeling a mite frail, Jesse, to be sitting up with her and you'd not want to lose your son, now, would you?'

'Of course I wouldn't! What d'you take me for? I'll do my bit, and I daresay Meg and Bessie would do a share of nursing.'

'Oh—Meg Conroy doesn't quite like me. I can tell.'

'You can't have it both ways, love.'

'You're right, Jesse. I should be looking after meself. Putting me feet up—'

'I'll see Meg, then.'

So it was settled and between them, Jesse and the Conroys took turns to sit with the sick girl until the inflammation was improved and it only meant rest and recuperation after the pain and fever. This, however, took several weeks and even then Clemence was pale and silent.

Although Jesse had decided to himself that his niece must holiday at Peel, somehow, once she was on her feet, Erin, having increased in size and diminished in patience, made it plain that she could not any longer look after husband and home.

The new, hard Clemence with the hooded eyes and cold profile did what was expected of her with little questioning, though her fingers were thin and almost transparent. It was as though, crablike, she had grown a shell which no one could penetrate.

If her eyes ever flared into life it was when Luke appeared, however briefly, in the distance. But, since most of his free time was spent down in Castletown, there were no more of those unexpected meetings.

Luke was playing the waiting game with Jenny Qualtrough and they said her father had taken a turn for
the better.

Clemence permitted herself a wintry smile. They
said everything came to those who waited. It might
even happen to herself.

* * *

Gowns and rings with green stones were not gained
by the production of the usual rotation of crops and a
bit of pasture for the pig and goat. The sheep belonged
to the master, as did the not too fertile land and Jesse's
annual and inescapable dues.

They were to drain the Curragh and introduce new
sheep to implement the loaghtyns which declined
through inbreeding, though the Lords of Man would
always wear the familiar fawn wool made into coats
and breeches, and not only because the weavers
required the support. No other material was so soft
and warm and pleasant to wear.

They said there was a snuff box in the House of Keys
made from the skull of a loaghtyn ram, and Sir William
Hillary had all four horns of one splendid male made
into receptacles for powder for his fowling-piece.

Many things were projected for the future of the
island but most were so embryonic that they would
not immediately help Jesse keep the love and interest
of his tantalising wife.

Clemence had experienced a relapse of her illness,
that, though not so serious, had necessitated rest she
could not have with Erin so demanding, and Jesse had
sent the girl to Peel for a few days to stay with her
aunt. There would be little rest for Clemence once the
child came.

On the day they had expected the girl's return,
Brand had called to say that the Peel carrier had left a
message that Clemence was to stay another week at
her aunt's insistence. Erin complained loudly and

Jesse could not blame his niece for preferring the peace of Deborah's quiet cottage.

Erin had become queer and unpredictable in these last two months of her pregnancy, half-turning against him and her isolated life at Croggan. If gowns and a circle of gold would warm Erin's coldness he would do anything. She did not get on with Meg Conroy and Johanne Karran got on with nobody. Erin was lonely.

Jesse would wake up in a cold sweat after nightmares in which Erin went away, leaving no trace. Last night he had run through a bone-white wood where green gowns dangled from stark branches, tangling him in their folds as he pursued his wife's shadow. A cat with glass eyes watched him.

The cottage had lost its neatness and cosiness and he never had clean clothes. The porridge was usually burnt and turnips half-cooked. And to make matters worse, the seas had been running unnaturally high, so that it had not been possible to uplift the precious merchandise that would earn him good silver with which to indulge Erin and make her more amenable. He had his own venues for the brandy and tea and bales of silk. Ravensdowne House would always accept illicit luxuries delivered at the back door, provided he accepted responsibility for any slip-up afterwards. The boat from Cumberland would come soon with its promise of reward. All he had to do was to row out one moonless night and bring back the highly-taxed goods that were so prized by the local gentry.

All his forbears had been smugglers and all had evaded justice. The luck would not run out with either Jesse or his son. Erin was so sure it would be a boy.

Sunday night was the third in the month and the time he was to look for the light from the *Glass Lady*. Erin was tired and cross and Jesse saw her to bed before taking Fiddler and the horn lantern from the stable and riding like a madman for the path above Bay Stacka. There was that dizzying track from it to the little boat that had been his father's and was always kept well-tarred and in a good state of repair.

Fiddler had been left securely tied in the copse, his panniers of suggane removed, and Jesse scrambled down the cliff path, lamp and tinder box ready. He saw the blink of *Glass Lady*'s light halfway down and rejoiced. It was the work of minutes to float the boat after signalling from the rocky shore. He pulled out strongly towards the darkened hulk that blotted out the stars.

Ellis was waiting, a shower of sparks falling from the clay pipe he tamped energetically.

'You'll deliver tonight?'

'Tonight.'

'Be back before sunrise. I dursn't linger. Not with Captain Jayce at Castletown.'

The contraband swiftly stowed aboard, Jesse struck out towards the cove. His blood pumped powerfully as it always did on these occasions. It was small crime really, not much more than pilfering, but all the excitement of a major operation was there. There were still bands of Manxmen in quiet places who ganged together, but Jesse was a lone wolf like old Sam Kinrade, his father. One man would not draw attention. Several horses left at the cliff top would spell out guilt.

He filled the straw panniers he had left behind a rock and hung them round his neck to leave his hands free. Fiddler whinnied softly in the dark and trotted on muffled feet towards Ravensdowne and then to Greys. Whillan was always last. Then, his pockets jingling with money, Jesse returned, tired now, but buoyed up with the knowledge that there would be some surprise for Erin to lift her from her depression.

His reward was a little larger than he'd expected and Jesse, pleased, realised that he could afford a ring, not that he'd dare purchase it on Man and have questions asked about the source of his unaccustomed wealth. He described what he wanted to Ellis and asked him to fetch it from Carlisle when next he came.

Whistling softly on his return home, Jesse wished that he did not have to wait for a month to lay hands on Erin's present. But it would be closer to the child's birth and a fitting thanks for her labour.

He slid from the saddle, groaning but pleased with the night's work, and entered the darkened house just in time to hear Conroy's cock crow three times.

* * *

Erin's hand about the house was heavy and unwilling and Jesse could not help moments of real vexation. Island women had always seemed to cope with their everyday lives in spite of childbirth. He had come to regret Clemence's departure and wished that she were back. The running of the cottage had been so smooth and effortless. Now there was only chaos and neglect and yesterday he'd noticed that the treasured blue and white plates were dusty and bore traces of spiderwebs.

When he had remonstrated, Erin had wept noisily and stuck out her belly to accentuate her condition. 'How *can* you scold me and me like a mountain with *your* child?'

'Others manage.'

'But I'm not a peasant—'

'So you're a lady because you didn't lie in ditches to pleasure your lovers.'

Her eyes widened and he saw that they were purest green. And very angry.

'I've never mentioned the women you've had.'

'That's different.'

'It's always different, isn't it! But I did have standards.'

'Aye,' he said drily. 'A bed instead of a field. And that makes it a horse of a different colour?'

Half of him was enjoying her rage, the other was asking desperately why he sought to hurt what he loved.

'I hate you, Jesse Kinrade! Hate this house and not having anything pretty. Hate having no one to laugh with. I was brought up with two sisters and two brothers and I like to hear things around me! People enjoying themselves—'

'The Conroys—'

'Are smug and dull.'

'Clemence never thought so. At lease, she never said anything.'

'I almost wish she were back. I'll never manage once the child's born. I know it.'

'Don't take on so. Please, Erin. I do my best.' He wanted to tell her about the ring but if he did, it would cease to be a surprise. Ellis was expected any day.

She collapsed against him, crying, and he held her close, stroking her red hair.

'There, there. It'll all seem better soon. The good weather coming. The baby here.'

'I'll not manage,' she repeated obstinately.

'All women do when it's their own child. And I'll do my bit for my own boy.'

She gave him a tear-drenched look he could only describe as strange, and smiled wryly where he had half-expected vituperation. 'If I could only go to market. It's cheerful there and I'd be with other folk.'

If he was hurt that she preferred the company of others, he did not show it. 'And so you shall, my darling. Once it's over.'

Privately, he wondered how he would stand that last month or so. His work on the land was arduous, with little reward. He was taking the weight off his wife's shoulders. And there was Ellis to contact this coming Sunday. Another lost night.

Not for the first time, he pondered about the man from Cumberland. He had many irons in the fire, obviously, to make his visits worth while, but managed to keep every transaction apart from the rest. What the right hand does, never let the left hand see. That was Ellis in the middle of his spider-web. He'd be taking goods out of Man as well as bringing them here to be distributed by his anonymous minions. There'd be gentry on the mainland wearing suits of loaghtyn wool as well as the Lord of Man.

It was fine on Sunday and Jesse breathed a prayer. He shaved at Erin's steel mirror and saw himself bright-eyed and well-groomed, still able to keep his wife in thrall. But for how long?

Long before it was time, he was putting the straw panniers on Fiddler, fetching the horn lamps, riding between the high, concealing hedges towards the moor that led to Bay Stacka. The sun was setting on the horizon and the sea was flooded with rose and silver. *Glass Lady* was a dark speck between sunset and land. How good it was to be alone, pitting his wits against the likes of Captain Jayce, looking him straight in the eye on market day and trying not to laugh.

When *Glass Lady* was closer, Jesse rowed out between the treacherous rocks that Ellis and his men could never negotiate safely. The Sugar Loaf towered out of the sea, a humped silhouette below the Chasms. Should he fetch Clemence back? More to the point, would she want to come?

Ellis had the ring. It was a pretty trinket, the two green stones set at a slant, one more brilliant than the other. There was a bolt of material that would make two gowns for the time Erin regained her figure. She hated being misshapen though he gave it scarcely a thought. It was not just her body he wanted.

All the way to Ravensdowne and the other houses where he was awaited, he pictured her delight and his own reward, though he'd have to wait for that.

He arrived back at a house ablaze with light and from which Erin's screams emerged, sharp and high as gulls' cries. Meg was there in the new bedchamber and his wife was lying with her knees drawn up and terror in her gaze.

'It's come too early,' Erin gasped between her pains.

Meg looked sceptical and Jesse was reminded of Erin's 'mistakes' in counting. He shut his mind against the suspicions that would poison their relationship.

He had time only for a bite of porridge before he had to go out to the fields. Meg had promised to send Bessie the minute anything occurred and he saw the girl from a distance, struggling towards him. He dropped everything and ran.

'It's a boy,' Bessie gasped, holding the stitch at her side. 'A fine boy.'

Exulting, he raced back, and pushed open the door. Erin sat up against a clean pillow, her eye sockets a little darkened, her expression composed. She had the child in the crook of her arm. If Jesse had hoped to see evidence of the boy's paternity he was disappointed. The infant was as red-haired as his mother and had an Irish cast of features. And the fond look Erin gave her offspring aroused a jealousy that disturbed him profoundly. A husband must expect to share a woman's affection once she had children who needed her love and protection.

But it was not the first time he'd had to buy her favour. Jesse produced the roll of creamy-coloured stuff and put the minute draw-string bag on the patchwork quilt.

Erin gave a little scream and pushed the wrapped infant into Jesse's arms. He felt awkward, holding something so small and helpless. There was not the joy he had once expected in the feel of a creature so alien.

The ring had fallen onto a patch of green spattered with white stars. Cupidity lit up the eyes that today matched the stones in the ring with a devastating accuracy. 'Oh, Jesse! Jesse, love.'

'Like it?'

'Course I do. And this'll make lovely gowns. Oh, I would like some little gold earbobs. And a watch.'

She prattled on and Jesse was suddenly deathly tired. It had been a mistake to tell her about his sideline, but she had to know what kept him from her bed. Erin was always concerned about what went on between the sheets.

'We'll see,' he said and put the child back in her arms.

'At least I can sew,' Erin went on cheerfully. 'Good

81

at that, I am. Now that I'm thin again, I can wear a pretty gown and go to market.'

'If anyone asks about the ring,' Jesse told her, 'it was left you by your grandmother. Understand?'

'Course I understand. Aren't you pleased I'll look nice again and that we can do things you've had to miss lately?'

Visions of Erin wooing him overcame the flatness of his spirits. 'We didn't have to wait as long as you thought.'

'No.' Erin did not look at him, only smiled vaguely into space, then held up the hand with the ring on it. The other arm was around her red-headed boy.

There were privileges that sons did not have, Jesse thought a little grimly.

'Can't we get Clemence back again?' Erin demanded, not without a trace of petulance.

'Only if you treat her properly.'

'And why shouldn't I?' Erin, in high good humour, looked as lovely as an angel.

'I'll see what I can do.'

'Just think, another few days and it'll be the same as it was.'

'Oh, Erin.'

He knelt at the bedside, the prisoner of his own weakness, and she ruffled his dark hair carelessly.

CHAPTER THREE

Clemence had as usual travelled back to Port St. Mary with the Peel carrier. The short stay with Deborah had calmed and refreshed her. Her mind was still charmed with pictures of the thin, gentle woman with the silvery eyes, the white cat and the cottage set in the secretive woods. Bottles with the afternoon sunlight shining through coloured liquids. Dried, unidentifiable things. Peace— She loved and looked forward to her periodic visits.

Setting her face against the wind, she began to walk along the cliff path from the village. The sea was high, crashing over the rocks in creamy cascades. A big house stood above the little bay that was dominated by Shag Rock. For the first half-mile, she had the feeling that she was followed but whenever she turned her head, uneasily, there was nothing to be seen but windblown bushes and dancing sea-pinks.

Passing Ravensdowne, she entered the glen that lay just beyond the cottage on the outskirts of the grounds. She did not hurry. This was her last taste of freedom for some time. If it had not been for her love for Jesse, she wouldn't have left Peel. Deborah had been quite content for her to stay. But Jesse deserved better than that greedy Irish scold. He had looked so tired just before Clemence left for her necessary visit.

She loved the wooded glen with its tumbling stream and the birdsong that echoed in the haunted aisles. If it had not been for that conviction that something, or someone, dogged her now hurried footsteps, she would have been almost happy. She could never be really carefree, of course, for, although the deep wound inflicted by Luke three years ago had healed over, the skin was paper-thin and could bleed again and again when her thoughts lacerated it. Just as she would never be free of her bond with Jesse, so too would she be bound in perpetuity with Luke Karran. He'd marry that shopkeeper's daughter in spite of the fact that he wanted herself more.

It would do no good, Clemence told herself desperately, to torture herself with such sweeping assertions. Luke cared only for himself and she should be glad he had shown himself in his true colours before she had committed herself irrevocably.

She whirled quickly, convinced she was not alone and saw Luke, huge and predatory, against a gap in the trees. Her heart leapt and her head felt suddenly light. She struggled against the incipient faintness. He had done this once before, with shattering results. Now, her strength depleted by the long walk from Port St. Mary, she could never fend him off.

The tall figure moved against the greenish-lavender of the wood's shade. Then the bushes and branches seemed to fly up into the air, sickeningly, like monstrous birds and she was falling—falling—

Luke caught her just before she reached the ground. She was light and boneless as a half-starved cat. Remembering why she was so fine-drawn, he permitted himself a flicker of remorse. Sometimes a man had to be cruel. But now that she was quiescent in his arms, all of the old magic was stealing back. Clemence had none of Jenny's bridling shrewdness. The tantalising glimpses that were all he'd had of her since Jesse's wedding, had pricked at him like a goad. He could not remember the last time she had been forced to speak to him, her voice like driplets of ice or venom. And the periods she spent at Deborah Quine's were a subtle torment. Not even the sight of her to alleviate the harshness of his working life. Jenny's voice and increasing demands bruising the memory of delicate eyelids and sweeping lashes, the pale, sunlit colours that were Clemence's essence. The scent of wood-smoke tangled in the fine strands of her near-white hair.

He could have her now, that dark urge was whispering. But that was not the way to the purest satisfaction. He wanted her alive and stirring beneath him, wanting him.

Luke cursed himself for not having gone to Croggan by the high route. But, seeing Clemence as he left the Qualtroughs' back door he had followed her as one might a will-o-the-wisp.

He wished he hadn't thought of Qualtrough's. It was so nearly his. He couldn't lose it now. Perhaps Clemence would be content to be his mistress. But Jesse and the Conroys would not allow that. They'd find some way of removing her from his influence.

Hungrily, he feasted his eyes on her as he followed the path, wishing she'd return to her senses. She must be mad for him if she could swoon at the mere sight of him. If she didn't recover, he'd have to make some explanation. But he'd done nothing.

She moved and gave a little kitten-like wail. Another moment and her eyes opened. She struggled feebly, then pushed against his chest.

'Put me down.'

'Not yet. I like carrying you.'

Clemence bent down suddenly and bit at his hand. Surprised, he let her go. She recovered her balance and began to walk away, white-faced and trembling.

Droplets of blood appeared round the tiny indentations of her toothmarks.

'You've made me bleed! Perhaps I'll get rabies,' he shouted, stimulated by the encounter.

'I wish you would.' She turned round to face him. 'Can't you see I don't want you following me and spying on me. I don't want another girl's leavings.'

'Who said anything about being Jenny's leavings?'

'Well, why are you pestering me, Luke? I was taught

85

that you can't have your cake and eat it. If you're so set on Miss Qualtrough and her lovely bricks and mortar, not to mention her nice, fat purse, you're welcome. You're too greedy.'

'I wouldn't be the first.' He laughed, then went on more seriously. 'You haven't forgot me, have you. No more than I have you.'

She became even paler. 'But I haven't a flourishing little business, have I, Luke! No shop and no little house to go with it. No windows overlooking Castle Rushen and the masts of Kerruish's boats. That's what you're set on. But there's more to marriage than being cock on your own dungheap. You may feel very big and important behind your own counter and adding up the day's takings, on nodding terms with the rest of Castletown's business folk, but your profitable wife isn't going to keep you obediently at home of nights because I know you too well. There's not going to be that kind of happiness, the sort another person might give you—'

'You, I suppose?' He sneered then and smiled arrogantly, then glanced beyond her with a new look that held what Clemence could only construe as fear. At the same moment she heard Johanne's voice, thick and furious, just behind her.

'*Not* you, Clemence Kinrade. You're bad for my son. I saw that the first minute you came, the first moment you were with Luke. I saw your dead mother, wrapped in sea-tangle, then I saw the shadow that filled the space between you and him. A cruel, bad shadow, growing, reaching out to swallow him, and I swore you'd never have my boy—'

'She was only twelve—' Luke began, but Johanne stopped him with a flash of her black eyes.

'She's death to you as she was to that mother of hers, such another pale, sickly creature at that.' Johanne transfixed Clemence with an accusing finger. There was a trace of froth on her lips as she spat out the words. 'Killed Lily Kinrade, she did.'

'How could she? And all those women there—'

'She knows. Look at her, Luke! See the guilt?'

Luke stared. Clemence bit her lip and looked away.

'And if you take up with her, she'll put death on you too. Folk that girl loves come to bad ends. Lucky she don't love too many. There's her uncle and aunt, and there's you. Just heed my words, Luke. Let her get her little claws into you and I see nothing ahead of you. Only a long, empty, echoing nowhere. Hell would be better.'

It was Luke's turn to change colour. 'I still don't see how you can be so sure—'

'I'm sure, all right. I got the power, Luke.' Johanne's voice was terrible, a sing-song so unnatural as to belong to a stranger. The dark eyes were mesmeric.

'Leave him be,' Johanne went on, returning to her own self. 'Just let him be.'

'That's what I have done. For three years. It's Luke —persists.'

'I told you, Luke. If you won't listen—' Johanne turned and went away, leaving girl and man rigid and silent.

The long moments passed, then Luke laughed uncomfortably. 'You needn't heed her too much. She thinks she can do things no one else can. I never really believed it—'

But Johanne *did* know, Clemence thought. Lily had died because of her own act. Only she'd never hurt Jesse and Deborah. She couldn't. Johanne was just a wicked and strong-minded woman who was jealous of anyone who ran after her precious Luke. As if anyone could destroy someone like Karran! She could almost laugh.

'And I don't believe it either,' Clemence said quite calmly. 'It's not because of that I'm asking you again to leave me alone. I'm going home now and don't you follow.'

'Don't give me orders!' Luke shouted after her as she took the opposite path to the one Johanne had taken. It would mean a long detour but she wanted to be alone. She must compose herself. Erin would be sure to notice any difference in her manner or appearance. A pity she didn't notice the slovenliness and muck around her. Poor Jesse. Clemence began to wonder if he thought it had all been worth it. Bodies didn't last out as long as the spirit and that's all Erin was. A body. And a complaining voice—

Slowly, Clemence's pulse stopped racing. The effect of Johanne's dramatic outburst drained away, leaving her faintly amused. Luke had some of that same enjoyment of the theatrical. And oddly, that wound hadn't really re-opened, only smarted a little.

She was over Luke. Thank God—

* * *

Clemence could hardly remember what Peel had been like. But at least it was peaceful which was more than one could say about Jesse's house. Little Boyce Kinrade had been followed ten months later by baby Elizabeth and Erin had grown increasingly lazy and unwilling to perform her duties as housewife and mother.

Jesse was patently unhappy, but he was still under his wife's physical spell and could refuse her little when she was in a good mood. Nothing pleased her better than to leave the babes with Clemence and to go with Jesse to market. She would wear her best gown and wash and brush her magnificent hair until it was a riot of soft curls. The little gold earbobs would gleam in the sunlight. Jesse had tried to warn her that to wear the jewellery in Castletown would only draw attention to himself and Captain Jayce was reputed to have spies everywhere. 'But they belonged to my grandmother!' she would say maddeningly and flaunt the bits of gold anyway, whatever he advised.

Barney Kerruish had not ceased to admire Erin. If anything, he looked more besotted than at the beginning. Jesse, who had at first laughed at the man's enslavement, no longer found it amusing. Erin sometimes smiled at Barney and he would doff his hat from the other side of the quay, his round face colouring with pleasure.

She had gone to the gates of Barney's boat-yard, surveying the great bustle and activity of making stocks and carrying planks, the hammering and transporting. From fishing boats, Barney was progressing to small schooners intended for European trade. He had not needed to struggle like the Peel shipwrights, who, because the river estuary was always filled with small craft, had to build their boats inland, then haul them all the way to the beach, a gargantuan task.

Always, when they returned from market, Erin usually carrying tributes of green ribbons or new stockings, Jesse would make violent love to her. That was one area in which Mr. Froggie Kerruish would never be able to shine and it was as well to remind Erin of the fact as frequently as possible.

Clemence would be there with a meal prepared and the two children usually fretful for their mother or grizzling with teething troubles, the cottage clean as Meg Conroy's.

'You used to enjoy the market,' Jesse said. 'A pity you miss it now.'

'Oh?' Clemence was not forthcoming. Luke Karran went to Castletown and she would die rather than be near him. In all the months she'd been back at Croggan she had never looked his way.

She had grown much prettier. Deborah had shown her the preparations that would make her hair shine and fall into pale waves after washing. Her face had more character and her eyes seemed bluer. She had put on a little weight in the right places. If she had not needed Clemence so badly, sometimes Erin could have been really sharp with her for having improved so greatly.

Erin professed not to notice that Clemence was often worn out with doing the lion's share of the work, but Jesse was uncomfortably aware that this was so. He had brought the girl back from the haven of Deborah's undemanding life to resume her life as his wife's skivvy. It was not right. A man should expect certain services from his woman but Erin recognised nothing but her own comfort. She would smother the children with caresses they did not understand if it would have the effect of directing Clemence towards a chore she abhorred. It seemed that she liked nothing that would make his home more comfortable. If he were not so happy in bed, he would have taken a stick about her shoulders. But she was so adept at gratifying those senses over which he had no control. Her slightest touch was enough to make him responsive. He had begun to dislike the person he had become.

Jesse knew that Clemence had returned because he had pleaded with her and had looked so like her father that she could not refuse him. She also had a love for children and caring for Jesse's offspring would seem almost like regaining little, lost Samuel. She had not forgotten her own family.

Reality was not as Jesse had pictured her return, but Erin dared not go back to her initial hostility for fear of losing her unpaid housekeeper and nursemaid.

Clemence now realised her own value.

Hugh still hankered after her and Jesse was happy for them to walk through the glen together when both had finished the day's work. He obviously thought that if Clemence lived close at hand, once wed, Erin would still have her mainstay and life would be simpler.

Clemence drew closer to Hugh Conroy during those happy excursions, for he was cognisant of everything that happened in the glen, where each animal lived and which bird frequented the copses, which plants grew, and when. She'd had time to overcome the wounds Luke had inflicted in rejecting her for Jenny Qualtrough and the Castletown shop. But his voice still haunted her in the small hours when she sometimes lay awake. 'Like a bit of a moonbeam, you are. See you at the Midsummer junketing, eh?'

Three Midsummers had come and gone since then. Her heart still turned when she caught a glimpse of him but she had never betrayed the fact. Just lately, he had seemed to want her again. Twice she had seen him from the small window of Jesse's cottage, leaning against the dilapidated wall, his dark eyes fixed on the door. She knew that she was easier to look at now that she had developed, and Deborah had taught her a few womanly tricks. But Hugh would make her his entire life. Luke? His eyes would rove again as soon as he'd had her. It was terrible to know it, yet be unable to exorcise him.

She had imagined herself safe on market day. Luke enjoyed Castletown as well as anyone and she'd watched him go off with Johanne and Aggie who looked crazier than ever. Queer blood there was in the Karrans.

Clemence took the children to the copse for a picnic, a treat they loved. Elizabeth was becoming the image of her mother and as charmingly selfish. Boyce was extrovert and handsome. They toddled across the dell glowing like two little sun gods, all red curls and beaming smiles. Usually they cried.

The unaccustomed warmth made Clemence languorous. The infants could come to little harm for they liked to stay within reach and they'd remember the small treats associated with outdoor meals. Clemence closed her eyes and listened sleepily to the children's chatter. There was a smell of spring flowers and old leaves.

She was startled out of her pleasant somnolence by a shadow blotting out the delicious heat. Clemence sat up, her heart thudding. Luke was staring down at her, his dark face all planes and angles, his cheekbones set above dark hollows.

Instinctively, she pulled down her skirts and touched her pale hair.

'Why aren't you at Castletown?'

'I had some sowing to attend to.'

'You went together—'

'As far as the north field. I've finished now.'

'I want you to go.'

'The world's free. Why should I?'

He sat down close by and whittled at a stick with a sharp knife. The children came and watched him from a safe distance. 'There, baby,' he said and threw the small wooden doll towards Elizabeth.

'Want one!' Boyce demanded jealously.

'All right.' Luke rummaged for another dry stick. 'Will you meet me at the Festival this year, Clemence?'

'Why should I? I've been caught like that before.'

'This time I mean it.'

'I'm not interested.'

'No?'

His eyes were drawing the soul out of her body. 'Hugh taking you?'

'No. Hugh's not going as far as I know. Neither will I.'

'Oh, yes, you will.' He tossed the second peg-doll to Boyce and came close to her. 'I was a fool last time. But now you've come back so nicely grown and so pretty, I've quite took to you again, Miss Kinrade.'

Pain and longing fought for supremacy. 'How can I believe you!'

'This might help.' He grabbed her roughly and crushed his mouth against hers. The branches above her whirled and vanished into a green-gold blur. Aeons later, the world steadied. Boyce was plucking at Clemence's skirts and Elizabeth chuckled at the doll she still held.

'Come,' Luke whispered and the whisper was more compelling than a shout. 'Forget Johanne and her awesome warnings.'

'I'll come.'

He moved away, smiling, sure of himself.

I won't go, Clemence thought without conviction. This time I'll let him down. It would serve him right.

She picked up Elizabeth as if in a dream, forgetting that they were to eat in the copse. Forgetting everything but Luke's kiss and his hard, faintly goat-smelling body.

* * *

She had supper with the Conroys a few days later. Erin had not wanted her to go but Clemence had ignored all the references to the hardship Erin would encounter with the children being so restless and herself so tired. They were her own babies, Clemence told herself and Erin didn't really deserve such bonny and attractive mites.

Once inside her neighbour's pin-bright cottage, Clemence acknowledged her own feelings of guilt. She had promised to do something she knew could only end in one way and that would hurt everyone who loved her. Especially Hugh.

She had become very fond of Hugh since her initial anxiety over his declaration of love. Often, her only refuge from strife with Jesse's wife, and her attempts to bring up Jesse's children in spite of their mother, had been Hugh with his unfailing kindness and real devotion. Clemence did not like to think of his reaction to the possible outcome of her intention.

Now that Jim suffered so badly with his rheumatics, Hugh worked doubly hard. He was a good son and would be a dependable husband and father. Good and dependable were not the adjectives one would apply to Luke. Luke was—exciting. A torment—

'You're not eating a thing!' Meg complained.

'You've got awfully thin lately.' That was Bessie, full of concern. 'Why, a breath of wind would carry you away.'

'I'm tired,' Clemence admitted. 'The children—'

'You do too much,' Meg said forthrightly. She had a smudge of flour on her cheek but no one remarked upon it. Somehow, that perpetual powdering was Meg's trade-mark and she would be incomplete without it.

'Jesse said you'd be over at Peel again for the Midsummer Festival,' Hugh said.

A great wave of colour swept Clemence's face and

93

ebbed away as quickly. 'Yes. My aunt would like me to go. I've never been there for the fair. She has—many plans.'

'You should go over, Hugh,' Meg suggested. 'Aunts are all right in their place but it's a man a girl wants at such a junketing. We could spare him just for a day or so, couldn't we, Jim?'

'Aye. Bessie'd help out, wouldn't you, lass?'

Clemence's head began to throb and she clenched her hands under the shelter of the table. It was all going wrong but she had known from the beginning that it would. Sun and music and Luke were being transposed into a shattered dream and reliable Hugh. That was unkind. When was worthiness a second-rate quality? Someone should thrash sense into her. Everyone had warned her about Luke. Jesse, Meg, Hugh and even Johanne, his own mother.

'I couldn't,' Hugh said regretfully, after what seemed like an eternity. 'I just couldn't spare even that long. Not that I won't regret that decision.'

Clemence smiled brilliantly and breathed once more. Her colour had returned and she began to enjoy the simple meal. Every now and again, the desire to laugh bubbled up in her. How terrible to feel such relief over Hugh's projected absence. It was obvious her fundamental reluctance to marry him was unaltered for all the improvement in their relationship. Why couldn't she break free from her obsession with Luke, for that was what it was? Marriage to Hugh meant a continuation of this evening, concern, gentleness, consideration and a timeless affection she knew instinctively would not alter.

When she rose to go, he went with her as was his custom. Outside, he said, 'I haven't changed.'

'Changed?' She pretended not to understand.

'Don't play games,' he replied more firmly than he might have done a year ago. 'You know well enough. The one occasion when we quarrelled.'

'Oh, that.'

'Yes, that. I still love you. More than ever, if you want to know—'

'And I feel as I did then. I want more time to think. It seems I'm not meant for loving.'

He kicked at a stone. 'That's nonsense. There's a kind of love that comes after marriage. Liking is a good start.'

'I like you almost more than any man I know. But something tells me that isn't enough. Not for me.'

'Oh, well.' Hugh's smile was crooked. 'You know where to find me when you give up your blown-up dreams.'

'It isn't that I think myself too grand—'

'I was teasing. Good night, Clemence, and don't let Erin put on you.'

'I'll have a rest—quite soon.'

'At Peel. I'm going to miss you.'

'Three days! Anyone'd think it was a lifetime!'

'It can be when you're in love.'

It was true. She thought she understood Hugh better in that moment than ever before.

Erin had not been pleased that Clemence was to go back to Peel for even a few days. She was pregnant again and disinclined to put herself out caring for Jesse and the children.

'I can go for good,' Clemence reminded her with surprising firmness. 'I just come back for Jesse's sake and the babies. I've only asked for three days.'

'If you must.' Erin gave in with ill grace.

'I must.'

Jesse was pleased that Clemence was to have the brief holiday and that he'd been able to supply the stuff for a pretty white gown dotted with palest blue and a length of blue ribbon for her hair. He affected not to notice Erin's sourness. Once Ellis had brought the little watch he'd asked for in place of his middleman's dues, she'd come round and be her generous, loving self. But, a watch took months of acting as a go-between, and he was only too human.

'Never did trust that Deborah Quine,' Erin muttered

after Clemence had taken the children out. 'If she'd lived a hundred years ago, she'd have been tossed into the Curragh Glass, or pushed down the side of Slieu Whallian in a barrel full of spikes.'

'Erin! You almost sound as if you'd enjoy that.'

'It's true. Just as Johanne Karran would have been burnt at the Market Cross in Castletown. She brews medicines out o' them purple berries and the laburnum seeds, and I've seen marks on the stones outside her house. Many's the time I've thought to bleed her nose or put rowan over the door. Why'd you think I sprinkle ashes and let that weed grow? The one with the yellow flowers?'

'You can leave that black cockerel be,' Jesse said harshly since he was not in Erin's good books. 'Next time I won't have one that's black.'

'Only you bought him before I came. They're best against witches.'

' 'Tis only old wives' tales! Who could fly on a broom or a pewter tray? It's nonsense, Erin. I thought you more down-to-earth than that.'

'It's fairies in Ireland.'

'And Man.'

' 'Twas the Irish brought them over. You'll be saying next, you wish I hadn't come at all!'

'I'd never say that, mavourneen.'

'Mark my words, she's up to no good, your saintly niece.'

'Clemence?'

'Aye. Your Clemence.'

And Erin went back to the chores she detested. Surely there was more to life?

All the way to Peel, Clemence lived through her projected meeting with Luke.

She'd help herself to one of Deborah's philtres so that Luke would need her so much that he'd forget Jenny and marry her. And she'd look for St. John's wort for a luck charm. True, it seemed that mugwort was to replace that, but the old ways were surely best? It had been Diana's day once but the Church was always set on replacing the pagan festivals with those supposedly Christian. Not that they'd be able to stamp out all the frolics in the heather, the dancing round the fires of bracken and fungi and dried roots.

She wondered if Deborah had gathered primroses this year and scattered them in the deep ruts of the lane. Of course she had. It was custom and the little people loved it. Like using water violets to improve the eyesight and banish toothache, and powder of ragwort to clap on a festering sore.

Clemence remembered all those evenings when there were knockings at the door and Deborah had answered them on low-voiced requests for potions to accomplish this and that, some for love, some for abortion, many for fertility. Most for love—

The money accrued from these always anonymous transactions bought seed for the vegetable patch, and oatmeal for the larder, fodder for the cow and goat, the hens that provided the eggs for supper and a meal at Christmas and feast days.

She'd be better off staying permanently at Deborah's, except that Jesse was so like her father, Joseph. They could have been twins. And she had worshipped Joseph.

The now familiar landmarks were full of a kind of meaning and glory. Perwick Bay and Port St. Mary, the turning to Four Roads Cross and beyond to the dark, fierce hills and the hostile moor. Dalby Mountain rose baldly above the trees of Earystane.

At the cairn by Kerroodhoo, they stopped to rest the horses and Clemence drank her bottle of buttermilk and ate the oatcakes Jesse had put in her pocket. They tasted good in the winey air and the breeze put colour into her cheeks.

Afterwards the cart climbed until they looked down on the greenness of Patrick and Glen Maye, crossing the turbulent river that emerged at the coast. Raby Moor came and went, Knockaloe engulfed them and receded while the sea was whipped into white horses. They crossed the Neb, Fiddler's hooves ringing out hollowly and the cart wheels rattling the wooden bridge with its glimpses of near disaster.

They slipped and slithered down the bank that led to the first thatched cottages of Peel and a loud outcry of gulls from the wide crescent of beach that lay, washed clean by the outgoing tide. Smoke rose from rooftops and made a shadowy mystery of the great red castle that straddled the island across the sand-bar. Clemence had grown to love the huge, sprawling edifice with its firelit window-spaces and implacable stones. The smell of fish pervaded everything.

Herring boats huddled in its lee, their colours fast fading with the dusk that approached. Children ran shrieking down alleys no wider than a man.

Appletree Cottage, where Deborah lived, was down a narrow, overgrown track. Water whispered alongside. Stunted fruit trees crouched close to the tiny dwelling with its minuscule windows and low, rose-hung porch.

Deborah opened the door and the white cat sidled out with her, weaving and posturing against her legs. Her hair was as pale as Clemence's and her eyes two rounds of water with no colour. But there was warmth in her embrace, and she had food ready on the table and the kettle suspended over the fire.

The low room was as strange as herself. Herbs hung, dried and shrunken, from the roofbeams. A great vase of honesty almost obscured the window and bottles and jars of liquids and powders filled the shelves. Potions and philtres for lovers and cures for coughs. Nothing like Johanne Karran's belladonna and laburnum seeds.

The watery tea tasted odd. Perhaps Jesse had given it to Deborah and she'd kept it overlong, having no visitors but herself. And then Clemence wondered if there had been something else in the delicate and not displeasing brew because she was talking more freely than she'd ever done and the room seemed, mysteriously, to close in on itself, all the bottles and dangling drynesses, the papery discs of the truthfulness plant, the birchlike slenderness of Deborah, pressing around her like a comfortable silvery womb.

Content and pleasure seemed to flow through her so that there were no problems that were insuperable. The dark image of Johanne was a pale smudge, her words forgotten. It was not true that all the people she loved were doomed to die horrible deaths.

'You're a woman now,' Deborah said very softly so that her voice merged with the silken cocoon in which Clemence seemed wrapped.

'I'm in love.'

'I knew. I sensed it the minute you came.' Was there a touch of fatalistic sadness in that whispering voice? Could Deborah have glimpsed that shadow she was supposed to throw?

'There's love towards you. I can see that. Like a warm blanket.'

How hot the room seemed to be, yet when Clemence looked, the fire was not large. The heat made her languorous and receptive, seeing new beauty in ordinary things.

'There is a man who feels so. But there's another—'

''Tis all mapped out for you. You must enjoy it while you can. 'Tis what we all must do.'

'I want the second to love me. Sometimes he does, then he turns cold.'

'Men can be cruel.' The bone-white fingers came out of nowhere and stroked Clemence's hair. She closed her eyes and the fingers felt oddly fleshless, yet no less indulgent. 'You can't change that. But it's not only men, is it.'

'There's women like Erin. She's like a poison that'll kill Jesse.'

'Folks are made cruel by others. A mother finds it hard to accept her child. It, in turn, will find it a burden to love others. Some never take to another living soul and die empty.'

'Oh, I don't want to be like that! Do you ever want to know—how you'll die?'

The silver silence stretched out. The white cat uncoiled itself and stared with eyes grown large as oranges. Deborah stretched out her other hand and stroked the creature's head. The sound of its purring filled the room with an odd, machine-like intensity.

'Some things, it's better not to know.'

But she knew! Clemence was aware also that Deborah had seen the manner of her own death but her tongue froze when she would have asked.

'I—don't know why we speak of dying. It's a cheerless topic when you're young and a great experience lies ahead of you. You'll find something at St. John's, something you've desired from childhood. But I can't yet see what lies behind it. There's gaps—long tunnels. Echoes. But that's not what concerns you, is it, my pretty.'

'I want to be beautiful for tomorrow. Jesse gave me the stuff for a gown. It's there, in my bag. But I want to put all thoughts of another girl out of—a certain person's head. It won't happen if he's half-hearted. I know that about him.'

'And that will make you happy, will it?'

'As far as I can see, there's two kinds of happiness. A short, sharp, painful kind and the sort that goes on like a garment you favour and don't want to wear out. Is it bad or greedy of me to want both?'

'Not bad. Just—human.' Deborah laughed a little sadly. 'Perfectly natural.'

'Then—help me to look my best.'

'You won't if you lie sleepless so I'll make you a potion.'

'It won't make me so sleepy that I'll not wake in time?'

'No. But I'll be up anyway. Always am at cockcrow.'

The potion was faintly bitter and was not long in taking effect. Clemence undressed sleepily, watching Deborah hanging up the new white gown. It swayed in a draught from the window, pure and virginal—

Now the walls were stretching away to infinity and she was floating with them.

Clemence woke to cock-crow and Deborah standing over her with a cup of the strange tea. 'I've a gift for you. These kid slippers. You've none to go with the dress.'

The girl was delighted. 'I'll go barefoot till I'm near St. John's, then they won't spoil. And now you must help me to look my best, as you promised.'

Deborah was pleased to help her. She gave Clemence a salve for her work-reddened hands and a cream to blot out the incipient freckles. She washed the girl's hair so that it was pale as straw and soft as silk and smelt delicious. Clemence stood in the stream and soaped herself all over and looked like Ophelia with the wild flowers all around her and the water dark as kingfishers' wings. Finally she swallowed the philtre. It would take effect later.

Kirk Maughold was a good place to be on a Feast Day but Luke would be at St. John's and therefore so must she. Slieu Whallian would do for Clemence Kinrade, frowning as it did above the village of St. John's and the Tynwald Hill with its acres of bracken and heather and plumy trees.

Wearing the white gown proudly, Clemence left the cottage, watched by the green-gold eyes of the white cat, and tied a rag to the tree beside the holy well as she passed. Deborah's face was a silvery blur inside the tiny window, like a piece of honesty set obliquely.

The deemsters were all on the green at St. John's when Clemence arrived two hours later, her feet sore and dusty but elegant in the new slippers. Luke was not there and her heart plummeted. There were folk in plenty, dressed in their best, enjoying the side-shows and buying from the stalls that surrounded the grassy space where the Tynwald stone took place of honour. White cottages gleamed in the sunshine and the heat was enough to tire anyone. There were flowers in the tiny gardens, the colours plucking at the unwary senses. But no Luke—

She saw him arrive, his tall figure dwarfing the rest, his black eyes searching the crowds until he spied her in one corner of the field. Everyone looked at him. How could they help it? The philtre melted her blood and her bones until she could not resist. First it was a powder in a jar, next it was the gateway to only Heaven knew what. Or Hell. She was sorry she had conjured up a vision of Hell while she was in such a blissful state. Luke took her by the hand and began to walk her away from the press of people, the noise, the outbursts of laughter.

They climbed and looked back at the kaleidoscope of dots that made up the crowd. Luke stroked at her wrist and sent frissons of delicious coldness up and down her spine. The bracken grew taller and she could no longer see the gathering below, only the towering summit and bald stones of Slieu Whallian. She shivered suddenly and Luke caught her to him, pressing her back into a bed of green fronds and purply foxgloves, stones that made her cry out. He seemed not to notice her cries, being intent on plucking at the little buttons that closed her bodice and the fastener at her narrow waist. His lips opened hers.

The sun was an enemy, draining away the marrow of her bones and drowning out the more prudent impulses of her brain. Clemence was aware of Luke's mouth being in other more intimate places, her own whispered protests ignored, the weight of his body forcing itself into her sheltered narrowness. His hand silenced her scream.

A strange pleasure crept through the pain. She pulled him closer, swamped by the heady rhythm of his body's movements. There was no earth, no sky, nothing but Luke.

She shuddered uncontrollably and moaned. No vestige of the potion's effect remained and Luke still invaded her like a Viking of long ago. She struggled against his strength and potency but he paid no heed. The glittering remnants of her ecstasy dulled into chips of dirty glass. The pebbles ground into her flesh. Then the backwash of her brief pleasure seeped along the channels of her nerves so that a pale echo of that glory remained until Luke straddled her, prostrate and gasping, his hands clutching at her hair.

'Luke?'

He did not answer.

'We'll wed, won't we?'

Luke grunted what she took to be an affirmative and buried his face in her breast. The fact that he obviously intended to make love to her again told Clemence all she so passionately wished to know. He still wanted her. It would be all right. She hadn't expected instant perfection.

They danced later on the green with the firelight on them and Luke looked at no one else. There was a green haze round the moon and the white gown had both pink and green folds as she moved, slow with lassitude and fulfilment. No one would know what had happened but herself.

Her lips clung to his as they parted.

'See you tomorrow on the road home,' Luke said.

'Come with me.'

'Best not. Your aunt wouldn't wish that.'

'I love you. Do you love me?'

'Wouldn't have said I'd see you here, would I, else?'

'I suppose not.'

Clemence would have lingered, bathed in the afterglow of consummation, knowing that there would be no sleep. She'd have liked too, to talk about what had happened, lovers' talk, lying close somewhere warm and private. But nowhere would be quiet and secluded on Midsummer Night, and she could see that Luke wanted to be on his way.

Doubts came swiftly. He'd not regretted it, had he? But no one could have simulated that violence of passion. It had been real, almost ruthless. And she'd gloried in it.

'Good night, then, my love.'

'Good night.'

He didn't kiss her, only walked away into the night without a backward look. Clemence did not move until all sight of him was gone.

CHAPTER FOUR

It was late when Clemence got back to Deborah's house. She had taken off the kid shoes after parting, unwillingly, from Luke. Deborah was asleep and Clemence lay down without undressing, reluctant to relinquish the gown, her body tired but her mind vibrantly alive. Part of her almost doubted that magnificent appropriation of herself but her aching flesh remained sufficient proof. The thought of Luke was a drug she did not want to do without.

She wished he had offered to see her part of the way back to Peel but that seemed not to have suited him. 'By the Cairn near Kerroodhoo, tomorrow then,' she'd suggested, warmed by the recollection of the second and third time he had possessed her. The magic that had somehow ebbed from their initial mating was there later in full measure. Clemence had not wanted the long, lovely night to end.

'By Kerroodhoo,' he agreed, and then had left her too summarily for her taste, but it had been very late in spite of the distant music and the faint shrieks and cries that still echoed around the Tynwald stone.

He was not there when she arrived at the appointed place next day, after being given a lift by the farm cart that had uplifted her three days ago, the farmer a friend of Jesse's on his own way to and from the junketing.

She could see for miles, across Barrule to Foxdale where the mines were, down to Glens Rushen and

Mooar, and behind her, Niarbyl Bay glittering in the silver light. The heat of yesterday was gone and she shivered in the clothes that were thinner than usual. It was odd that Luke was not here when he had a shorter distance to come.

The light faded after a time and it began to drizzle slightly. The great southern peaks turned purple, then a watery grey as the haar increased. Deep in her bones she knew now that it was useless to wait for Luke. He had overslept or met someone who could put some lucrative business his way. It would be foolish to linger. Pulling the inadequate shawl over her gown, she began to hurry in the direction of Ballagawne and Port St. Mary.

She was soaked by the time she reached home and Jesse was worried in case she had been set upon by drunken tinkers.

'I tried to shelter,' she explained, 'but there's little cover.' At least the disagreeable journey would account for the dishevelled dress that Erin was scrutinising with disfavour and curiosity.

It was as Clemence was sitting with her feet in hot water and mustard, the dress lifted to her knees, that she saw Luke through the window. Her heart somersaulted. She was so intent on the sight of him that she was unaware of Erin saying sharply, 'There's blood on your undergarment.'

The second time, Clemence did hear and her stomach muscles twisted. 'It's the curse. It came on me unexpectedly.' Her voice was surprisingly calm.

'You had it a fortnight ago.'

'Surely it was more?' The girl's voice did not falter.

Erin, who had seen the look Clemence had given Luke, held her tongue. Jesse had come back into the room and he'd not thank her for continuing the conversation. Funny how men hated any mention of a woman's courses, particularly when it was they who put a stop to them.

Clemence spent the next few days fighting off a heavy cold and aching for Luke to think of some way they could be together. Erin made it impossible for her to contrive a meeting and she'd die if she had to wait much longer.

Market day dawned and Erin itched to go to Castletown. Luke had not been near the place and she thought she might have been mistaken in her suspicions. Anyway, the children would keep Clemence busy enough as Elizabeth was particularly fretful in the heat. The town would be so delightfully busy. Not like Croggan—

Clemence waited until Jesse and his wife were safely out of the way. Earlier she had glimpsed Luke going up towards the north field where the oats were ripening. Carrying Elizabeth and with Boyce toddling at her heels, she walked purposefully through the drifts of long, scented grass, revelling in the sweetish perfume.

Luke was working, bare to the waist, his splendid chest and shoulders golden-brown. Colour flooded the girl's face as she remembered Midsummer Night. She'd been shameless. But she'd do it again a thousand times if it would keep him in love with her.

'Luke?'

He turned swiftly and she could have sworn he was angry. The brief emotion died.

'I haven't seen you since—St. John's. I waited up at the Cairn.'

'I couldn't come.'

'When can I see you?' Her eyes were full of pleading.

He shrugged and all the muscles under the tanned skin moved smoothly and with infinite grace. 'There's much to do. You can see for yourself.'

'I know Erin watches me but I could come out after they're in bed. Luke?'

His eyes narrowed and his mouth was cruel. 'We had our fun that night. But it's different here. Jesse—'

'Won't know, I promise!' His indifference was striking at her heart, every part of her. Knife-sharp jabs that made her want to cry out. But hadn't she begun to realise already that he could have come to her if that

106

was what he'd wanted, and had pushed the painful knowledge to the back of her mind?

He turned his back on her and picked up the hoe. 'No, Clemence. And please don't come bothering me. No mooning about our place.'

It was as though he truly had struck her. He was not to be bothered and she—what was she to do with the rest of her life? The moon had been hazed with greenness. And his body—his beautiful body had been part of her own.

'Dolly,' Boyce said. 'Dolly. Where's my wooden dolly?'

The colour had drained from her face. If she had not had the children with her she would have thrown stones at Luke, made him take some notice of her, even if he beat her to death for it afterwards. The well-muscled arms went on with their task. She might not have been there. She wanted to die—

'Your doll's at home, Boyce. We'll go there and look for it.'

'Yes. Mama made a dress for it. White with little blue dots. A bit left over from yours.'

She hated the gown. She'd burn it if there was a fire on, only it was too hot for fires. But she could cut it in pieces. Little jagged pieces.

She looked back once but Luke was still working, still half-naked. Still indifferent. He'd had his fill of her on Slieu Whallian. Whatever it was he had wanted, whatever desire there had existed was dead as burnt-out ashes. He had not troubled to conceal the fact.

He belonged to Jenny and his ambition.

'My dolly—'

She forced herself to patience. It was not the children's fault that her life was in ruins. But she'd make him pay one of these days. One day she'd have her revenge on Luke Karran. But it hurt. How much it hurt!

* * *

It was August by the time Clemence knew what was wrong with her.

'You're pregnant,' Erin accused. 'It's that randy goat next door.'

'You were pregnant when you married my uncle,' Clemence stated flatly.

'What's that? The wicked lies!' Erin was white with shock and fury.

'Well, don't expect me to go lying down outside,' Clemence mimicked with devastating accuracy. 'I only does it indoors.'

'You bitch!' Erin screamed and set the children off crying. 'I knew all along you were up there, all ears!'

'I've only known one man and I'll never care if I have another,' Clemence said bitterly. 'But I'd be glad to be spared your hypocrisy.'

'Oh!' Erin could think of nothing else to say. At the moment.

Later, in bed, she informed Jesse of Clemence's condition. 'I knew it. I saw her petticoat while she steeped her feet and there was blood on it. It was the wrong time of month.'

Jesse was horrified. The girl was in his care and it must be his fault for not being more vigilant. 'It must be Hugh Conroy. But I'd never have thought—'

'Don't be a fool! Can you imagine Meg's darling putting himself out to pleasure a woman! He's not a man. It was Luke. Plain as the nose on your face.'

'How do you know?'

'He was away at Midsummer. And I've seen her look after him.'

'He must wed the girl, then.'

'And how will you make him! She'll not say, and he'll do nothing, you see.'

Erin was right, of course. Luke disclaimed all knowledge of having relations with Jesse's niece. He was promised, he said, to a girl in Castletown as Clemence very well knew. Clemence, tight-lipped, refused to divulge the father's name. There was nothing Jesse

108

could do. But Clemence could read his disappointment and suffered accordingly. Erin's opinion was of no account.

'How will I manage now?' Erin demanded, patting her growing bulge. 'You're so generous with your seed, I'll be forever carrying your childer.'

'I've never noticed you refusing my attentions,' Jesse retorted, stung.

'Sometimes—'

'Well?' Jesse said, dangerously quiet.

'Oh, nothing. If there was only some little surprise—'

'You've had your ring. Your ear-bobs. Dresses. Ribbons, stockings—'

'I know.'

'And God help me if Jayce finds out where they came from. There's nobody will say they *asked* for the goods. It'll all come back on me.'

'I'll be careful.'

'Careful? You don't know the meaning of the word? There you were, flashing them about at Castletown. After I begged you—And nobody knows who's Jayce's informant.'

'I'll not do it again. But, that Clemence. She'll be no use to me vomiting in the garden and increasing. You don't think she'd be better off with Deborah?'

Jesse swallowed the words that rose to his lips. His marriage was the biggest mistake of his life. But when Erin was malleable as she would be when the watch was his, it made up for the bad times. The watch! He'd have it next month.

'Leave things be for the moment,' he said harshly. 'She shouldn't be shuttled about just now. She needs us. Good God, woman, you've been pregnant yourself. Surely you've the imagination to put yourself in her place?'

'What do you mean, I've *been* pregnant? I am.'

'All the more reason to practise a bit of understanding then.' Jesse crashed out of the house and Erin, aware that she skated on very thin ice, prudently kept her own counsel for the meantime. At least there would be Jesse's next present to look forward to. He knew how much she set store by a watch. He'd get it somehow.

* * *

It was autumn when Hugh finally overcame Clemence's objections to becoming engaged. His heart had been wrung, first with a bitterness that she could throw away her virginity on a man to whom the sacrifice meant nothing, then with pity for a Clemence so pale and quiet, so obviously suffering.

The difficulties of living with Erin and Jesse must be considerable.

Hugh had won over his mother from her initial disappointment.

'But she let you down,' Meg had protested. 'She was —faithless.'

'No, Mother! Clemence never made me any promise. She was always honest. Several times she told me not to waste my time over her, that she didn't, and may never, love me. She thought of me as a good friend. That was all.'

'You never said so.'

'It was my business. And I still hoped I'd persuade her some day.'

'We all thought—'

'That's the trouble with well-meaning people. They always think.'

'That isn't like you, Hugh.'

'I'm sorry if I was sharp with you, but it's not easy watching her so downcast and miserable.'

'No, son. It can't be.' Meg's natural generosity asserted itself. She'd imagined that Clemence had led Hugh on but that wasn't so. Not that she'd ever envisaged Hugh wedding a girl six months gone. He deserved better than that. Still, he'd made his choice long ago and the Hughs of the world didn't change. And the family had always been fond of Clemence.

Meg decided she must bury deep that little flicker of distaste at the thought of the girl's wantonness. Erin must be as much to blame as anyone and Jesse had never been what one could call a saint.

Luke Karran had set a date for his own wedding now that old Qualtrough had finally gone to his eternal rest, and it was the sight of Clemence's face at the news that roused Hugh's protective instinct to its uttermost. This would be the time he would be most needed. If ever she were going to accept him, it would be now. Erin would be telling her the worst.

He had waited for Clemence to emerge from the house after the blow to any hopes that still might linger. It was always her habit to go out to think and to face up to matters.

No one would imagine she was pregnant, he thought, his heart quickened with love and apprehension. The cloak concealed everything. Her neck and white face rose from the buttoned collar like a snowdrop against the dark background of a frostless winter. They were the only pale things against December's greyness.

'Clemence?'

She stared at him almost unseeingly.

'I'll come with you.'

She said nothing, only continued to walk as if in a daze.

'Life goes on,' Hugh said. It was trite. It was a cliché. But it was true.

'Does it?' She gave him a small, dreadful smile and Hugh was impaled on a thrust of hurt.

'You know it does! And there's plenty of people want to help. I do, for one.'

'You've always been too good.'

She made it sound like a crime, or was he just being too sensitive?

'I wish—' She sounded softer, more approachable.

'What do you wish?'

'That it had been you I fell in love with, and not —him.'

111

'Then change your mind. It isn't too late. Show him you don't care. *That* would be a blow to his pride! Don't you see? He'd never get over it.'

'Yes, it would hurt him, wouldn't it.' Life came back into her voice and a trace of malice spiked her smile.

Perhaps it wasn't the best reason for agreeing to marry him, Hugh thought, but once she was his, love might follow. It wouldn't be his fault if it didn't.

'All right. I will marry you, but it's the same as before. Don't say I haven't warned you. I could make you dreadfully unhappy.'

'I'm an optimist,' he replied, swamped with incredulous, boundless surprise and relief. He'd never expected her to give in this easily. There was hope if she did want to dent Luke Karran's arrogance. For once he'd said the right thing.

'Kiss me to seal the bargain?' He didn't wait for her acquiescence, but bent to put his lips on hers. Her mouth felt cool and soft. And quite untouched. He wondered suddenly how it had been that night she and Luke—Damn Karran to hell! It'd not have been like this, so cold and enduring. Hugh had never experienced anything like this vast, boiling wave of rage that must surely be plain and simple jealousy. He had not known it was in him. But if he wanted her he must learn to live with it.

They walked on as if nothing had happened. But the wood was unquiet with the violence of both their thoughts.

* * *

Luke could hardly believe it. He'd fully expected Clemence to come to him, pleading with him to change his mind, but instead she'd affianced herself to Conroy. She was all composure and scorn and derisive aloofness. And triumph.

It was strange how her new behaviour revived that old attraction. Not entirely, of course, because the fey enchantment had gone as soon as he'd possessed her.

Broken flowers and butterflies were valueless and Clemence, robbed of that elusive innocence, was like all the other girls he'd had. Prettier than most, but reduced to flesh and blood and lust. The image of floating lightness had forever vanished that night on Slieu Whallian, not that Clemence would ever have understood.

He might have gone on meeting her if he hadn't seen Jenny's cousin as they danced later on the green. If Bobby Qualtrough had noticed him, that would have been the end, for Jenny would never brook being second-best. The near disaster had sobered Luke. Clemence had become an embarrassment, especially when she found herself with child. If Jenny ever came to hear of that! But Clemence had kept her silence and the unpleasantness was past. Or so he had thought. He was safe, and in two or three weeks he'd be master in his own house down in the town.

Yet the thought of Clemence belonging to Hugh roused something in Luke that was totally unexpected. It was his child she carried. His body was the only one she had known. He'd rather she'd borne the bastard and stayed his for the rest of her life. That would have been her punishment for losing overnight the magic that had coloured his life for all those years, an enchantment he would never find again if he lived to be a hundred. Desire, resentment and a kind of hatred built up in him.

The sight of Clemence became an obsession. Now that she'd thrown in her lot with Hugh, she did not stay inside so much. He could see her every day, walking with the Kinrade children, the wind blowing the cloak against her body. That bulge was his child, a baby that would become Hugh's once they'd made their vows. It was odd how jealous he was that he could never claim it. His own flesh and blood. He did not want another man to father it, yet he was powerless to prevent both girl and infant belonging to a man he'd always despised and detested.

How ironic, that now he was only a stone's throw

113

from achieving the ultimate in ambition, he was beset by devils and useless regrets.

Returning in the afternoon, Luke saw the sun turn red, bloodying the water of the stream. Clemence had just come out of the cottage, her pale face incarmined by that winter splendour. She had not seen him. Somehow, the sight of her brought all those uncomfortable currents and eddies of feeling jostling to the surface. Though he was tired from the day's work, all thoughts of rest and food vanished. He must speak to her. Deflect her from her intention to wed Hugh.

She was lost among the bare trees. He hurried after her. How swiftly she walked in spite of the burden of her pregnancy. The dark flutter of her cloak was the reverse side of the long-ago witchcraft that was composed of sunlit draperies wafted on summer breezes. He had a sudden image of her eyes, so huge and blue and intent, swallowing up her face. Black cruelty rose in him like bile. She should not be casting spells on him. He had far too much to lose.

His tiredness made Luke careless and Clemence had heard him. The look she cast over her shoulder betrayed her fear.

'Clemence! I want to talk to you.'

She responded by increasing her pace until she was almost running.

'Clemence!'

He had lost sight of her and the track divided at the edge of the wood. The crimson sun had poured itself into the sea while a wedge of a moon was climbing up into the scudding cloud. She'd be making for Spanish Head.

Luke crashed through the tangle of roots and shrub. The trees were black plumes like the ones on horses he'd seen at a Douglas funeral. Before him, the track lay deep and moon-washed towards the Chasms. She was a black, moving blur not far ahead.

'Clemence?' She'd taken the wrong fork in the dimness.

Something in the timbre of his voice had made her run, stumbling in the dry ruts.

He caught up with her, gasping, and grabbed her by the arm. The smell of peat-smoke rose from her hair. Her flesh was warm and firm under the stuff of the cloak.

'Don't marry him,' he said roughly.

Surprisingly, she laughed. 'Hugh was right. He said that was the way to get the better of you. He's obviously not such a fool as you imagined.'

Luke squeezed her arm painfully. 'I'll not be laughed at.'

'You're hurting me.'

'I'll hurt you more if you go through with that wedding.'

'But you don't want me. Why shouldn't I have some happiness? I can't see Jenny sharing you even if that was what I wanted, only it isn't.'

'It's my child—'

'Oh? That's not what you told everyone. It was someone she picked up at Peel, you said. Some sailor from a herring-boat— Remember? You—betrayed me.'

'Be quiet!'

'I'll not! In two weeks you'll have gone to Castletown and I'll be with Hugh, free of you at last, and my child will be his. He wants it.'

'I could kill you—'

'I wish I'd not wasted all that precious time—' Clemence whispered.

'Loving me? You still do.' He saw through all the vengeful defiance.

'I was thinking, last night, that I had a perfect name for my baby. It would suit either a boy or a girl. Karran. That should make people think.'

'You wouldn't.'

'There's nothing to stop me. I swear now, on my mother's soul, that I'll do it. And I respect her soul—'

'You bitch! Jenny—' Love and necromancy were forgotten.

'I care nothing for her. And neither do you if the truth were told. Let her suffer for a change.'

Luke lunged towards her. His mind throbbed with anger. Clemence started back when she saw his expression and ran further along the narrow track. As she heard his feet cracking the dead heather roots, she screamed, aware that she had gone too far. It was darkening and it was lonely and Luke had a need to humble her. To have her crying out for mercy. To sully her so that she'd turn from Hugh in a revulsion for all men.

He was gaining on her and in her agitation she had carried on beyond the point of safety. A maze of little tracks ran across the heather webs of the Chasms. 'Don't be a fool, Clemence! That's dangerous.'

'Not as dangerous as you are.' The moon, brightening, cast her small face into a mask of beauty.

He'd been wrong to cast her off. The layers of indifference were peeling off and he remembered all the sensations of that summer night. Then he recalled the threat. Jenny would be bound to hear the child's name eventually and discover that its mother was Jesse Kinrade's niece. She'd remember seeing Clemence at the wedding. Jenny was already jealous.

Worse still, there was nothing to prevent Clemence from going to the shop tomorrow and confronting Jenny. There would be no marriage, no bettering himself. He'd be a laughing-stock as Hugh led Clemence from the church.

Moonlight drenched the narrow tracks that intersected the crevasses. He wanted to go after her but caution made him tread carefully. The main path was safe enough.

'Karran!'

The voice came from behind him. Surprise made Luke stop in mid-stride. He slewed round then started to laugh in disbelief.

Hugh Conroy stood only yards away.

* * *

Clemence had been so intent on Luke that she had not noticed Hugh's approach. All her emotions had been centred on Luke's big, arrogant form and the mixture of lust and hate that distorted his features.

Now that Hugh was there and Luke had switched his attention from her, she became intensely aware of her isolation and vulnerability. Spurred on by her fear, she had strayed too far and now her stomach revolted against the vertiginous sensation of taking another step to nowhere. She dared not move a finger.

Johanne Karran's words came back from the past. 'A long, empty, echoing nowhere. Hell would be better.' Johanne saying that people Clemence Kinrade loved came to bad ends. There was a curse on her. Here on the moonlit moor, Clemence believed that.

Hugh's voice rang out, hoarse and unrecognisable. 'Leave her alone, Karran.'

'And what if I don't?' Luke was still laughing. The lamb had turned on the lion with a vengeance. His whole body shook with the force of his mirth.

Clemence did not recognise the Hugh who flung himself at Luke, his fists flailing, his lips spewing out terrible accusations. She watched impotently as the two ill-matched figures came together, one still in the clutches of a rib-cracking amusement, the other shouting out the pent-up detestation of a lifetime.

She still loved Luke, of course. However bad he was, whatever he did, the inner core of her nature would always respond to his beckoning. But there was the terrible pity she had for Hugh. She was committed to him.

Luke's fist crashed into Hugh's face, sending him staggering, but he came back lurching and shaking his head. She would not have believed it of him, but then, what did she really know of Conroy? He must have seen Luke following her and realised that Karran meant her harm.

'She's a bitch,' Luke taunted. 'She'll come to my bed any time I whistle.'

Hugh rushed at him, grabbing at Luke's knees and bringing him to the ground. They rolled over and over, panting and cursing, the dried roots snapping like gunshots and stones set rolling into hollows.

For the first time she noticed the sound of the sea behind her. The calm swoosh of it running over the shore and the indrawn breath of its going hypnotised her. Its calmness was a mockery set against the brutality before her. Luke was rising to his knees, a boulder in his hand, and Clemence screamed a warning. Hugh moved but not quite fast enough. The big stone grazed the side of his head, stupefying him. She watched him crumple, lie still.

Luke stood up, dusting down his breeches. He was smiling, coming towards her.

'Luke?'

'I've a mind to have you,' he said. 'One last time—'

Still, she could not move or speak. She felt like a moth on a collector's table. Something ready to be impaled, stored away in a glass case to gather dust in the future.

Luke seemed to have forgotten everything but his compulsion to reach her. He was omnipotent, a tall tree of a man, his shadow reaching out for her as his arms soon would.

She shrank away from him instinctively. Johanne said there had been a shadow between them from the beginning.

Hugh was moving, groaning, getting up on his knees. 'Don't touch her—'

The unexpected sound distracted Luke briefly. He turned and in that moment, his foot slipped off the path. Half his leg disappeared into the loose heather. Frantically, he scrabbled for a handhold on the twisted roots. The weight of his body dragged at his other leg and he was sliding in to his waist.

Clemence saw his hands and wrists straining to retain their tenuous hold but the old roots were moving. Tearing, snapping off with spiteful little noises. Luke was submerged to his chest and his mouth was open on a yell she would never forget. Screaming still, he slid, with horrifying impetus, from view, his cries reverberating obscenely for a second. Two seconds.

There was a terrible silence that went on and on.

* * *

They were bound together in complicity. Clemence had lost her senses for a time. How long, she had never known, but when she was next aware, she was in Hugh's arms and in a place of safety. Crying, she had tried to return to the spot where Luke had fallen into the crevasse but Hugh, unexpectedly rock-like, had prevented her. The heather had sprung over it. They'd never find it. No one would.

'I don't want to live—'

'Of course you do. Would you deny your child life?'

It was part of Luke. Of course, she didn't want it dead. It would be a boy, just like his father. Dark and beautiful and compelling. And she'd sworn on her mother's memory and soul to call him Karran. How could she not?

Dark, beautiful—and dead. She could remember screaming, repudiating the inexorable fact, pleading with Hugh to help her, conscious of his arms around her, his voice soothing her terrors.

'It was no one's fault.'

'It was! There's a curse on me. I kill the people I love best. I can't help myself—'

'That's nonsense. Nonsense. We couldn't stop him.'

'The shadow. His mother saw it—'

'Johanne likes the feeling of being able to frighten the rest of us—'

'She was right. We didn't believe her.'

'She was lucky. That's all. What happened fitted her flight of imagination.'

'She knew,' Clemence protested.

Tenderly, he caressed her and supported her. She

119

did not want to leave the place but there was nothing they could do.

'They'll find out.'

'How?'

The stark question made her see that Hugh was right. If they both adhered to their stories no one could prove they had ever seen Luke tonight. What could be more natural than that they had gone walking together? The graze where the stone had struck Hugh was under his hair. If he did not draw attention to it, no one would notice. And luckily, the place where Luke had hit Hugh with his fist was under his chin and the skin was inclined to blueness there in any case. If he neglected to shave for a day or two, it would never be noticed.

'But it was an accident,' she whispered. 'Why do we sound so guilty?'

'You know why.'

Johanne. She loomed large in both their minds. Johanne—

'Hugh. I can't marry you immediately. I see that now. Luke was so angry about his child being yours. He could—influence—'

'Clemence! That's nonsense! He's dead.'

'Shush!' As if there was anyone within a mile of this dreadful place. 'When the child's born, I'll marry you as I said. It must have his name.'

'But it was to save you the censure—'

'I don't care about that now. Why bother to hide what everyone knows?'

He could not shift her over the matter any more than he could persuade her to go home again. Endlessly, it seemed, she stared over the Chasms as if trying to draw her lost lover from its deadly embrace.

At last, defeated, she allowed him to guide her back towards the copse and the track that led to Croggan. It was much earlier than either had thought. A lifetime had passed for both of them and yet it was only an hour or two since Clemence had left for her ill-fated walk.

They went to Meg's, for Clemence balked at facing Erin's shrewd gaze, and there they drank to the forthcoming nuptials and allowed themselves to become enmeshed in the web of familiarity.

It hadn't happened, Clemence told herself, bone-white with weariness.

But, of course, it had.

* * *

Johanne had searched for Luke but had found nothing. But she had been intimidating in her determination to find out what had happened to her son. She had stormed her way through Castletown in case he was at Jenny Qualtrough's and when he wasn't, she had walked every inch of the town, visiting each inn and brothel, without success. She had scoured the copse and the approaches to Croggan, all without finding any trace of him.

'Why should Clemence bother with him when she's to marry Hugh?' Jesse had enquired, reasonably enough.

Captain Jayce had come looking for him, his sharp eyes taking in the glints of gold about Erin's person.

'They were me grandmother's. She had a bit o' money,' Jesse's wife said glibly. 'She left me these ear-bobs, this ring—'

'Anything else?'

The green eyes widened. 'D'you see anythin' else, Captain?'

The captain had to admit he could not but his cold, chiselled features betrayed his dissatisfaction. Jesse could hardly conceal his perturbation at coming under the captain's microscopic scrutiny. He was angry with Erin after the captain had gone, for being so pert, and for drawing unfavourable attention to himself.

He regretted that he'd already asked Ellis to bring the watch. It could lead to nothing but trouble.

* * *

Meg had been unable to understand why Clemence should delay the wedding. One would imagine that Hugh's generosity would have been sufficient spur. But the girl was adamant that she go to Peel first and the Conroys must accept it as one of the unreasonable whims of expectant mothers.

'She'll leave it too late to make the child legitimate,' Meg told Hugh and, while she was not exactly asked to mind her own business, she was made to understand that it was Clemence's own affair. Of course, after Luke's mysterious disappearance the girl was bound to be upset.

Clemence was pale as a lily when she left for Peel. Jesse noticed how her mouth twisted a little as she looked back at the decrepit outlines of the Karran abode. The shadow of Johanne lay over the dirty window panes. Harsh sunlight outlined the near-white hair that escaped from under Clemence's hood and turned her blue eyes to living flames. It was as thought she and Johanne were engaged in some deadly duel and something momentous had passed between them.

Then the blue eyes were hooded and she presented a profile as cold as the weather.

Erin waved from the doorway and Jesse forgot his niece and Luke. The same light that emphasised Clemence's silvery fairness, made a glory of his wife's rioting curls. She was the most beautiful thing he'd ever seen and she was his.

It was hard to ride away, to lose sight of Croggan among the spindly trees of the copse. The sun became more brilliant and the glimpses of the sea a hard, bright blue. Though they had never talked about the reasons for Clemence's journey to Peel, to both, they were painfully clear. Quite simply, there was no room for both girl and woman in Jesse's home and while he could do without Clemence, he could not exist without Erin.

And for Clemence there was an additional reason.

The baby must be hers, nothing to do with Hugh. If it had not been for Luke's determination to prevent that, he'd not have died in that dreadful way. The memory still seared her mind so that she woke in a sweat of fear, his cold, dead hand laid upon her.

Deborah accepted the arrival of her niece with a pleasure Jesse could not deny. He had thought her a colourless creature, without character, but he no longer believed this.

Conscience pricked at him as he contemplated leaving Clemence there for her indefinite stay. Then thoughts of Erin rose up in him, erotic and compelling. The only way he could expect peace was to put Clemence aside. She'd be all right here with her own flesh and blood, until she married Hugh.

He left early as there was no room for him in the small dwelling. The last glimpse of Clemence, white and languishing after the long day, filled him with compunction, but her present helplessness was almost immediately blotted out by the memory of Erin's baffling and beautiful eyes.

Were they green or grey? He was never sure. He only knew that he could never do without her.

Once Clemence was with Deborah, she did not want to go back. She was safe inside the cramped little cottage with the bottles on the shelves and the dried herbs. With the woman who seemed dryer and more rustling than ever. Like a spray of honesty.

There were the same knockings at the door, the anonymous voices. Pleadings— She drowned in the greyness and mystery.

During the day she walked by the stream with the white cat for company. No matter how far she went, the cat remained, almost as though Deborah had ordered it to look after her. She smiled at the fancy. It was a long time since anything had amused her.

It was the cat who ran off the day she was taken with an agonising cramp and Deborah had come soon afterwards as if she'd been summoned.

'It's the child,' she said, after a hasty examination.

123

'But—it's not time.'

'It is for this baby. It's in a hurry to see the world, poor lamb.'

'He'll be all right, though?'

'Of course.'

She had supported Clemence along the January bank, as kind in her own strange way as Hugh was in his.

The goose-feather mattress had enveloped the girl, its softness in terrible contrast to the lacerating agony that engulfed her.

The baby was a girl. It was hours after the traumatic pain of parturition that Clemence knew the sex of the child. For a time her mind had repudiated the fact. She had sunk into a limbo where Slieu Whallian was a vague shadow and the only reality was a moon diffused with spectral green.

'What will you call her?' Deborah asked, her eyes silver coins.

'Karran.'

'What sort of name's that?'

'She needs it. It's her—protection. He'll not be forgotten. I won't let it happen.'

'It's her father's name, then.'

'Yes. Yes!'

'Have you looked at her?'

She had. It was Luke who stared up at her with infant eyes. The very planes of his face—the black, rumpled hair. Karran Kinrade. Of nowhere in particular. She'd have to fight for her place in the scheme of things, poor little mite. Clemence began to cry quietly.

It was better for her to weep, Deborah thought.

Slowly, Clemence became curious about what had happened at Croggan during her absence. Hugh was anxious for her return and she was promised to him. There was no going back on her word. But still she shied away from the inevitable wedding-day.

It was as if Deborah could read her mind. 'They'll want to see you. Erin—'

'She won't! All she wants is the strength in my arms for as long as they'll keep going.'

'The Conroys will naturally wish to welcome you.'

'Will they? Meg and Jim must have their reservations. They set—great store by me and I've spoiled all that. I missed Bessie's wedding. That was a pity.'

'Jesse, then. He'd want to see her and he can't get away now that he's three children.'

'I'd like to see the third.'

'James Kelly's going that way a week today. Why don't you beg a lift?'

'I might.'

Clemence did speak to James because of Jesse. But a coldness came over her at the cairn at Kerroodhoo and a terrible sadness as she stared across at Foxdale and then to Niarbyl Bay. She did not look at Slieu Whallian. The result of that summer madness lay in her arms, her dark little face proclaiming her sire as much as her name.

It was Johanne Clemence saw first as she came out of the copse, the child held against her breast. Ignoring the hostile gaze, she passed, head high, to Jesse's cottage, and knocked upon the door.

'Well!' Erin said, her dress and hair slovenly. 'I don't know how you have the sauce!'

Beyond her, Clemence could see a naked baby in a basket on the floor. A boy who looked as like Boyce and Elizabeth as a pea in a pod. He began to cry, his head turned towards Erin as though he could not exist without her presence, his arms imploring.

'What's his name?'

'Sebastian.'

'He wants you.'

'He'll have to wait, then.' Erin laughed without humour. The cottage was in a mess.

'Where's Jesse?' Clemence deplored the dust and neglect, the cracked plates on the dresser.

'In the pasture.'

All the way along the lane that ran between the Kinrade and Karran abodes, Clemence was aware of

125

being watched. Johanne would know that this was her first grandchild. Erin must be seething with spleen because Clemence would be spending the night, perhaps two, with her uncle and she could not forbid it.

It was hot and butterflies flitted between two buddleia bushes, delicate and beautifully marked. Like miniature paintings come to life.

She knew then why she had come, after all these months. The first glimpse of Jesse showed her a man subtly older and a little more care-worn. She had missed him more than she could express. She'd always love him, however weak and vacillating he could be, and wish to be near him.

Jesse saw her at the moment of truth and ran to greet her. He was still like her handsome papa, brown and bearded. She loved him like a daughter and regretted the fact that he was wasted on Erin Doyle who was a whore and a slut.

One look at Karran and Jesse saw what everyone else would see. That it was indeed Luke who had fathered the child.

Over tea, they chatted their everyday observations, not daring to delve beneath the surface, while Erin glowered in the background, Sebastian held in her arms, the only place where he would remain quiet. Boyce and Elizabeth were consigned to the loft where Clemence used to sleep. Tonight Clemence was to occupy the hole in the wall bed that was once Jesse's. She might have occupied it indefinitely if it had not been for Hugh. He had inspected little Karran with a hint of wryness she had not expected.

'Well. You made sure she'd not be my daughter, didn't you.'

'I couldn't help it.'

'We warned you about the journey.'

'I had to get away. That awful night—'

'Sh! Don't ever speak of it. Especially not here where Johanne is.'

'No. I forgot for the moment, but she won't harm Luke's child. She knows. I passed her yesterday and

126

saw her looking inside the shawl. Her eyes seemed to burn right through it.'

'She's just a strong-willed old woman.'

'Of course.' But wasn't there something else? She'd known about Lily and Luke. She'd described her son's death exactly. A two hundred foot tomb—Clemence shivered.

'Marry me now and I'll take care of you.'

What was the point in holding out? She'd never love anyone else and there was the baby to feed and clothe. Jesse had sufficient problems of his own. She was not cheating Hugh Conroy in any way. A cottage had just been vacated, not far from Meg and Jim. A good worker like Hugh would get it without trouble if he took a wife.

'I—I don't want any fuss like Jesse's wedding. I'd hate that.'

'It will be as you wish. That's all I care about.'

Meg had taken charge of Karran for the day while her son went to Port St. Mary to be wed. She'd like to have been there but it must be as Hugh wished. While they were away, she and Bessie tidied up the new cottage and decorated it with greenery, leaving food ready and a fire burning.

The baby lay in a rush basket and stared into the shadowy recesses around the roof beam with black, wondering eyes. Meg was reminded, uncomfortably, of a certain look of Johanne's. But there was no denying the infant was handsome. She wondered at Clemence's decision to call the child after its father, but wouldn't Johanne be inclined to respect the girl for the sheer effrontery of the action? After all, it wasn't as if there was any great secret about the tiny girl's paternity. She'd keep the baby tonight so that Hugh should have a proper wedding-night. Only himself and the girl who could do no wrong in his eyes.

What had become of Luke? Had he become engaged in a drunken brawl in Castletown and fallen into the harbour? Or tumbled off a cliff and been drowned? Set upon by tinkers and buried in a woodland grave?

There were still numbers of poor Irish arriving. Or had he simply grown tired of being torn between prospective wife and mistress? Taken a boat for some far place, maybe.

Meg lifted the basket containing the baby and let Bessie close the door. She prayed Hugh would never regret his insistence on wedding Jesse's niece. But a cold finger of doubt stroked her shoulder blades and made her shudder. They had not heard the last of Luke and she had the chilling suspicion that he was not too far away.

Hugh carried Clemence over the threshold. His heart beat faster than usual. Even in the dimness, the cottage looked friendly and once he'd put a taper to the rush lights he saw what his mother and sister had done.

The greenish light made a soft, unreal glory of his bride's hair. 'I love you,' he whispered, over and over again, disregarding the meal that was set on the table.

He had never made love to a woman before and his fingers were clumsy as he unfastened her gown and took her to the bed. Her body was the same mistletoe colour as the rush light. Beautiful and untouched.

But of course, it was not really so inviolate. Somehow there was another guest at the macabre wedding-feast. Luke was there, smiling from the rafters, laughing from the dark corners, mocking his every move. Hugh knew that he was awkward, that Clemence must be making her own unfavourable comparisons. Then, his desire overcame the feeling of being overlooked. Haunted. He must make her his own tonight or Karran would have won, and they'd never be free of him.

Her arms did not hold him tightly enough. Her mouth had not the response he would have wanted. But she did not push him away or refuse his advances. And the sensations that were aroused by the possession of her body were exquisite. Surely, in time, she would experience something of his own pleasure?

He had no lover's tricks, Clemence was thinking.

There was no magic. But there was kindness and concern. She too sensed Luke's presence but there was no guilt attached to either herself or Hugh. That had been an accident. If Luke had not insisted on punishing her, he'd still be alive, still vibrant with health and strength. Luke—

She tried to attune herself with Hugh, but it was not going to be the same. Consideration was never going to replace what she had felt on St. John's night. Diana's night. The enchantment of Slieu Whallian and a pale green moon would never be repeated. Never—

She thought she was going to cry but it would never do to show her husband her unhappiness. Hugh was the best man she had ever known. It was a very special night for him and she couldn't spoil it.

'I do love you, my darling—'

'I know,' she whispered. 'I know. It'll be different in a little while. You'll see.'

But would it?

* * *

Karran was growing fast. She could be, almost in the same breath, as ugly as a monkey or as beautiful as sin. Clemence, busy now with Hugh's babies—inexperience did nothing to stop the conception of infants—had little Joseph to care for and another child on the way. Hugh had almost forgotten that night at the Chasms but she had not. She was not yet nineteen but she had endured everything that could hurt and change a woman. It was an age since she had seen Deborah, and the shadow of Johanne loomed large in the small area inhabited by the Conroys.

Why, if Johanne had such powers, had she not understood what had befallen her son? Or did she know half of the dreadful story while the rest remained obscured?

Clemence had never heard of the Sword of Damocles but some retribution must surely follow.

Erin had given birth to no more children since

Sebastian. She had taken the advice of a wise woman in Port St. Mary and remained barren, which was just as well as three children seemed too much for her. Sebastian was like the other two, handsome and red-curled, but incurably besotted with his mother. If she went anywhere, he screamed and beat at the door until she returned. No one else could do anything with him.

Bessie was having a baby and Meg went often to the croft near the Calf to see her daughter and to give her sensible advice.

It was Bessie's father-in-law, Tom Quinn, who made the terrible discovery. He had gone to the moor above Spanish Head to round up his new stock of sheep. The dog was inexperienced and had directed one or two of its charges towards the Chasms. Sheep being what they are, without any sensory perception, they browsed alongside the dangerous tracks and one had fallen through the mat of heather.

Thomas could hear it moaning and could not bear the sound. He lowered a rope tied to a rock, and went down, hand over hand, a horn lantern tied round his waist, to put the beast out of its misery.

He came up faster than he had descended, very white of face and clutching a belt he had taken from the mouldering remains of a corpse on a ledge.

The whisper was soon around that the belt was Luke Karran's, as was the calf waistcoat and boots. What was he doing there? Luke had been aware of the dangers of leaving the defined track. The dread words foul play were pronounced. The parish constable and Captain Jayce came asking questions.

Clemence answered like an automaton. Hugh, alive to the dread possibilities, was infinitely careful. The night Luke disappeared he and his family were celebrating his betrothal to Jesse's niece. Yes, the baby was Karran's but months had elapsed since Clemence last spoke to Luke. Luke had made it plain that he had a fiancée in Castletown long ago. Meg and Jim, silent in the background, had nodded their agreement.

Captain Jayce found Erin surrounded by incompleted tasks and three children as handsome as herself. His sharp eyes noted the fob-watch pinned to her well-filled bodice.

'You said your grandmother left you a ring and a set of ear-bobs,' he told her.

'Did I? It's so long ago. I don't know how I came to forget the watch. It's been in me family for as long as I remember. I was her favourite, ye see.' Erin smiled insinuatingly.

'I see all right.' Captain Jayce, not being a fool, did not press the matter then and there. Jesse was within easy reach of the sea, owned a tiny boat that was once Samuel Kinrade's, and was also extremely fond of his niece and would take it badly that Luke Karran had both enjoyed Clemence, then repudiated her. He was not only a smuggler but he was a murderer. Lately, there had been reports of strange lights seen at Bay Stacka which was no distance from the Chasms and only a short ride from Croggan. There were moneyed estates not too far away, where brandy, wine and tobacco would be welcomed. The cold, analytical mind recorded the reasonable theories and made them fact.

Johanne had no such reserve. It mattered not to her that Meg and Jim Conroy upheld the story put about by their son Hugh and that white rat of Jesse's. That slut—

She put on her shawl and made her way towards the new cottage on the other side of the burn. She had chosen a time of day when Hugh and Clemence would both be at home. The toddler, Karran, was playing outside, and the child's likeness to Luke cut through her like a knife. The broom she carried became an instrument of vengeance. Cruel fingers tightened round the handle. She swept the dirt on the path towards the house, foam flecking her lips.

Karran cried out and Clemence, then Hugh, came to the door.

'I curse your filthy, whoresome bed,' Johanne whispered harshly, her eyes as hard as jet. 'I curse your

131

hovel and all that's in it. Your food, your garments, your abominable seed. I curse your goat and cow. Your hens and cock. Your crops, the growing things within your boundary. I curse your chance of happiness and success. And I curse all your children but the one that was my Luke's. Only she is left out of my curse. And don't think to have me made to do penance with sheet and candle for I'll deny everything, and I'll say the Lord's Prayer backward while I stare at your windows nightly! No good will come of your marriage. And I curse you most for being the instrument of my son's death. For you killed him. I know it as surely as I live, you whey-faced bitch! I knew you were trouble the moment I saw you. You killed my Luke. My only son.'

She flourished the broom and the dust rose in a great cloud, obscuring their white faces. Only Karran watched her with interest and composure.

'I'm your grandma,' Johanne whispered and leaned on the birch twigs, out of breath but taut with outraged grief. 'And don't you ever forget it. Never, do you hear? Never!'

Karran watched her sombre figure grow smaller and smaller, then vanish round the bend towards the tree-bridge. The flying leaves and debris slowed their wild dance and everything was still.

* * *

It hurt him to see the wreck Clemence had become. She was pale as milk and nervous as a newborn colt. Hugh was not much better.

Neither did Jesse care for the knowledge that Jayce had been to the house questioning Erin about the gruesome discovery at the Chasms. He'd be bound to notice the watch that Erin wore at every possible moment, though time meant little in a croft in Croggan. A watch was a sign of prestige and Erin had pretensions towards being a lady in spite of the lust that had drawn her to himself. If it were possible she'd have had a nursemaid for the children and a housekeeper to do the cooking and cleaning. If it had not been so serious, Jesse might have laughed and chivvied his wife out of her grandiose dreams. She could even regret not having accepted Kerruish's offer all those years ago. Barney had still not married and he always searched the quayside for the Kinrade stall, buying Jesse's produce in spite of the fact that others displayed goods of better quality.

Erin, in spite of her growing slatternliness, was still a beautiful and bedworthy woman. Kerruish, it was said, had made such satisfactory profit from his boats that he was considering leasing land Foxdale way. Mining could be very remunerative and he was unlikely to be able to expand his business in Castletown. More and more, Douglas was becoming the key town of Man, however Castletown might rebel. More industry, more building, more visitors. Better harbourage. More room for large ships and a bigger fleet. A unique position.

'A brooch,' Erin suggested when the Luke Karran business had blown over, written off as an unfortunate accident in spite of private thoughts and guilty knowledge.

Johanne and Aggie had gone early one morning after the verdict. The Christians at Douglas had told Jesse that they were seen going aboard the Liverpool boat, laden down with shabby bundles and hair like haystacks, bound for only Heaven knew where. But it wouldn't be Heaven—

They were cosily in bed and the children conveniently asleep with the aid of a little cordial obtained from the woman at Port St. Mary. Jesse would have had a fit if he'd known, just as he would have been furious about the bottle that kept Erin free of further childbirth. He thought it a cure for the indigestion that seemed to plague his wife.

'A brooch?'

'Ellis must owe you a fair sum by now. I'd so like a

brooch to match the ring. A green stone in it and tiny pearls.'

'Pigs might fly,' Jesse retorted, his heart beating. They had not yet made love together and he wanted her so badly.

Her body stiffened. 'It's not much to ask, Jesse.'

'And what's the captain going to say?'

'I'll not let him have the tiniest peep at it. I promise.'

'That's what you said about the watch.'

'I mean it this time.' Her eyes and her hair were so lovely in the candlelight. It was difficult to remember that she was past thirty and that she could be so cold when he balked her. She should be begging for clothes and boots for the children, not gew-gaws.

Her arms were around his neck and her breath on his cheek. Her body pressed against his. Hard to recall that she could be a shrew. How he wanted her.

It was a different matter next morning, his promise filed away in her mind like some immovable stone. His dividends were so small that it could take years to pay off the trinket that Erin envisaged. On the other hand, she'd be so careful to please him that it would be worth the worry and danger. He despised himself.

But the next time he'd ridden to the cliff above the cove he'd been overcome with such a presentiment of doom that he ignored Ellis's signal. There was something about the darkness and the suddenly accentuated night sounds that made his body cold. He had sat astride Fiddler and cursed his inability to light the horn lamp and make his way down the stony path. The track across the Chasms was silver, beckoning him like a skinny finger.

He had not told Erin.

Next month he took himself in hand. He'd tell Ellis he'd been ill and that he'd take twice as much as usual to make up for last time. It would slow him down but it was his own fault for giving in to fancies and cowardice.

It was very dark and if Ellis had not shown a light he'd never have known the *Glass Lady* was there. Jesse

134

lighted the horn lamp and swung it three times so that Ellis would recognise his signal. It was the same lamp his father had used and his grandfather before him. One day Boyce would want to use it.

The sense of disturbance that always came with the thought of Boyce was very marked tonight. Jesse could never rid himself of the conviction that the boy was the progeny of some Irish adventurer. Eight months children were always suspect, especially if they were smooth and perfectly formed, with all their fingernails. The thought of Erin with another man always had the power to hurt him. She'd not bothered to hide the fact that they'd existed but she knew him well enough to realise he'd resent her coming straight from one lover and foisting off that man's child as his own. And she had a weakness for Boyce. Poor Sebastian worshipped her but received not one quarter of the love that came his elder brother's way. Or was Boyce his half-brother?

Fiddler seemed restless but submitted at last to being tethered to a thorn. Jesse, weighted with suggane saddle-bags, began the steep, familiar descent. The yellow light played anaemically on the scored rock and the dried ghosts of seapinks. Dead bones of heather roots showed through dust. He had an image of bodies long buried, without any proper grave. Joseph and Lily seemed to beckon to him from the rocky beach.

Jesse told himself that he should be ashamed of such womanish fancies but the sound of a child's faint laughter echoed inside his skull. A stone rattled and Fiddler whinnied from the rim of the cliff.

Jesse pushed out the small boat and began to hum. The sound combated his irrational disquiet. Erin's demands precluded the possibility of giving up this lucrative sideline, but his nerve had gone. He went on rowing and whistling. The tune of "The Spanish Lady" floated across the oily swell, soft and evocative. It was a melody he'd always liked and it put him in mind of Erin. Erin—

He came upon the *Glass Lady* with a suddenness that

made his heart thud. A haze of tobacco smoke drifted across the rail where the light of the one shrouded lantern was shed. 'Ellis?'

'Aye. What happened last time?'

'I was took bad.'

'That's not like you.' Ellis spat over the side.

'No.' Jesse was climbing, hand over hand, and the sea made sucking sounds around the small boat. 'I'll take more this time.'

'Will you manage?'

'This one journey.'

Once aboard, Jesse made out the vague shapes of men by mast and rope, and tiny glints from the iron hoops round the barrels on the deck. There were smells of tobacco and rum and fish, of tar and salt. All the normal excitement of his night excursions began to return. It was warm and snug in Ellis's cabin and the sweetish odour of wine was comforting.

'Your dues,' Ellis said, his large, bearded face sweating, 'will you be wanting silver?'

'A little. But the rest to be put towards a brooch.' Jesse described the trinket.

Ellis grunted. 'Is she not content yet?'

'It's my own business, I think,' Jesse replied a little coldly, 'what I choose to do.'

'She's close-tongued, I hope?'

'She knows nothing but that I go out at night and that I am tired next day. I've told no one what I do. That's why I always work alone.'

Again Ellis grunted and shouted to one of his half-seen companions. 'Put double the usual in the bags! You'll break nothing, Kinrade? I can't pay for what's not delivered.'

'I'll be careful.'

'And don't be late in the morning. I've other deliveries to make and you know the time o' the tide.'

'Aye.'

He worried about the weight of the bags once he was back in his own boat. The rock climb would be a labour and it was too much for Fiddler. But he could

136

not afford a second horse. In any case that would cause comment in the wrong quarter. Even to borrow one would lead to talk. He'd be followed.

Jesse was halfway to the shore when the sky was split by a huge orange flash and for a moment *Glass Lady* was outlined, her black silhouette extraordinarily graceful, sails billowing gently. And then her mast was struck and the sails collapsed, sinking like tired bats. The air was filled with a confusion of shouts and crashes, an agonised scream. There was another explosion and beyond the bloom of fire Jesse made out the shape of another vessel, squatter and more powerful.

The Excise! Jesse struck out strongly. The cutter would be more concerned with Ellis's capture. They were, in any case, too far off to catch himself. He'd conceal the stuff in his little cache at the back of the beach and gallop for home. The hiding-place involved squeezing behind a huge boulder and it was known only to generations of Kinrades. He could leave the stuff there until the business was forgotten.

Panting, Jesse rowed until his wrists and shoulders ached. The glutinous sound of the water seemed louder than the noise from the two vessels. There was scattered gunfire but the shots were now those from muskets. Looking back, he saw that *Glass Lady* was ablaze at the stern. Little ropes of fire danced about the trailing shrouds. Splashes told Jesse that men tried to escape by sea. They would not be allowed to get far.

The hull of the boat scraped the shingle. Jesse forced himself to calmness as he tied the rope and lifted out the bulging panniers. He should have thrown the stuff into the waves, except that these goods would pay for Erin's brooch when the hubbub had died down. There'd be no more trade with Ravenglass or anywhere else.

Raising the lantern, he began to hurry over the shifting pebbles and rock slabs. Limpets cracked under his tread. He half-slid on a strand of seaweed and cursed beneath his breath, then regained his balance.

There was still another pannier to fetch. For a long moment Jesse rocked precariously.

Some sixth sense warned him too late that he was no longer alone. A hand grabbed his arm and the cold barrel of a pistol was pressed into his neck.

'We've been waiting for you,' Captain Jayce said very softly. 'I'm glad you've not disappointed us.'

'Damn you to hell!'

'No. That's for you,' the captain said more loudly. 'That's where you'll be when you've been hanged at Castletown. Aye, Castletown where your lady wife likes to show herself off. What'll she do now she won't have you? Eh? Tell me that.'

'Damn you!' Jesse whispered viciously.

'She'll have no trouble if she goes upon the streets. There's many a man wanted to lie with her and she doesn't look averse to fornication. Especially not if it's to put a little trinket on her hand or her bosom. I'd favour her myself—'

'Shut your mouth!' Jesse roared and dropped the precious burden. He twisted and ducked, his boots pulverising slivers of broken glass while the brandy ran off the rock slab to disappear into a myriad crevices. His fist caught Jayce in the midriff but he had no time to strike him again as the weapon exploded harmlessly.

Another pistol was raised and came down on Jesse's head. The night was gone on a train of stars and grinding pain.

* * *

Erin could hardly lift the lion's-head knocker for shaking. She'd had to bring Sebastian for he'd not have stopped crying till she returned. Twice, the heavy brass came down with a sound to waken the dead.

A plain but very clean maidservant opened the door, her eyes widening at the sight of the dishevelled woman on the step. 'You can't come to the front door—'

'Is Mr. Kerruish in?'

'Beggars go to the back—'

'I'm not begging. Mr. Kerruish knows me. He'll be angry if you send me away.'

The girl stood, irresolute.

'Who is it, May?' a woman's voice shouted from the back regions.

'Someone who says the master will be vexed if I don't let them in.'

'Ask them their name.'

'My name's Erin Kinrade.'

'I've never heard the master mention you.' The girl looked doubtful. Erin was as white as a piece of china but, in spite of her untidy appearance, she had an undoubted air. 'You'd best wait.'

The door closed. He must come and let her in, Erin thought with a mixture of desperation and growing excitement. He'd never allow her and the children to starve. Perhaps he could get Jesse out of Castletown jail? But did she really want Jesse released? She gasped as the thought became predominant. Without Jesse, she would be free. From the moment she was told of her husband's arrest she must have entertained the idea at the back of her mind. He'd never be let out. Jesse had been caught red-handed and had resisted arrest. And she'd not object to a release from serfdom.

The door was jerked open and Barney was staring at her as if at a dream. 'I thought May joked. That there was some mistake—'

'There's no mistake,' Erin said quietly. Tears of relief stood out in her large eyes. 'I was so afraid you'd send me away.'

'I'd never have done that. You must have known.'

'Can I come in, then? Sure and it's a long walk from Croggan, especially with me youngest so dependent on me.'

Barney flushed and stood aside. 'Begging your pardon, but I was so taken by surprise. We'll go into the parlour. There's a fire and I'll have some chocolate brought.'

She was inside a pleasant, well-furnished hall with a large oil painting of Manx boats with blood-red sails dominating one wall and a portrait of a rather frog-faced lady on the other. The resemblance to Kerruish was unmistakable.

'Is she your mother, now?' Erin asked, mock-innocent.

'Was.'

'Oh, I'm sorry.' She wasn't really. Mothers could be the greatest block to any sort of relationship concerning their sons, especially an only son. Erin had made her own enquiries about Barney long since. He had no brothers.

' 'Tis all past and done with. You've not raised any spectres, Mistress Kinrade.'

The parlour was filled with comfortable sofas and chairs and the curtains were of velvet. There were glints of brass and white china dogs with black spots on them that entranced Sebastian, who had lapsed into disquiet at the sight of a strange man and an unfamiliar house. He toddled straight for the Chelsea china, the firelight making a nimbus of his red curls.

'He'll break them,' Erin exclaimed, holding out chilled hands to the blaze.

'No matter.'

'But it does matter! Beautiful things should be looked after.'

'Leave him be. Now sit down and tell me what troubles you.'

Erin chose the green plush sofa that accentuated her pallor and the red of her disordered hair, the shade of her incredible eyes. It was as she had known for a long time. Kerruish was besotted with her. His hands shook as he lifted Sebastian back from the hearth. The child howled and Erin took him onto her lap. 'Sure, and he's very clinging. I'm the centre of his life. I can't think why.'

Barney obviously agreed with the infant.

'It's about me husband. He was caught smuggling and they've got him in Rushen Castle. Captain Jayce says there may be another charge besides the contraband.'

'That's very bad. The laws are very strict since the wave of unbridled smuggling some years ago.'

'A great man like you must know some important men. Deemsters and the like. If you could put a word in for Jesse. 'Twas only petty crime. A few bottles, a bolt or two of silk and damask. Tea—'

Barney had coloured at her description of him as a public figure. 'I've not much influence, Mistress Kinrade. Not that I won't speak up for you. But I wouldn't want to raise false hopes.'

'At the best,' she said quickly, her eyes filling very fortuitously with shining wetness, 'he'll be in gaol for years. At worst—'

'At worst?' Barney leaned forward, hanging on her words.

'He could—die. The captain did mention—hanging.' Erin's voice broke on a sob.

'Oh, no!' Barney, for all his penchant for Kinrade's outrageously beautiful wife, could look at such punishment only with compassion.

'Yes. He was carrying a fair amount of contraband. But there's something more. Something the captain only hinted at. I don't know what that is. And I've three children, Mr. Kerruish, depending solely on me and no home once the Master takes on another man. I need to have a roof and work of a sort. I'd do anything—'

'You poor child.' Barney was aghast. Of course at forty-three he was entitled to think of a well-preserved Erin as being younger than her thirty-two years. 'I'll do what I can, believe me.'

'You've a beautiful house,' she said wistfully, glad that her natural pallor made her the more pitiable. 'I do so enjoy pretty things around me.'

'You said Mr. Kinrade's Master's looking for a new man,' Barney said huskily.

'He must. The beasts must be taken care of and there's the field work. I couldn't—'

'Of course you can't, not with your responsibilities. There's no one local?'

'Only the Conroys and they have more than enough to do, though Hugh's feeding the beasts and cleaning the byres. There was Luke—'

'Luke?'

'Karran. But he fell down the Chasms—'

'Oh, I did hear about that. Found by Farmer Quinn.'

'That was the way of it. An accident, of course, though to hear folks talk we're a murderous crowd at Croggan.'

'Surely not!'

'Jesse's niece had a child by Luke. He could have killed him for that! Oh, my, it was only a figure of speech, Mr. Kerruish! It's all we've had to put up with since Quinn found him. The gossip and the sly looks—'

'I know. Will you promise me something, Mistress Kinrade?'

The enormous green eyes looked up at him trustingly.

'What? What must I promise?'

'That if there is any danger of your being put out, you'll come here? It's a big house and I'm sure some post could be found for you.'

'Established staff don't like interlopers, Mr. Kerruish, especially when they've a handful of bairns. But I love my children and I'd die sooner than let them starve.'

'You need not worry on that score,' Barney assured Erin. 'Anyone in this house without sufficient humanity to have sympathy for someone in your unhappy position would not be welcome in my home!'

'How good you are.' Erin buried her face in Sebastian's neck, knowing without looking that Barney's expression would be one of doglike devotion. How stimulating the knowledge of one's magnetism could be. She was as good as settled. There were things she

142

would miss if Jesse didn't come back, but at her age, a man who'd worship the ground she walked on and could afford someone who'd take the children off her hands, was better than finding a tin-mine. She'd not need to raise a finger. Steeling herself against a memory of Jesse, unshaven and shaken in a damp, barred cell under Rushen Castle, Erin said tremulously. "You're a saint. However can I thank you?'

'No need for thanks,' Barney asserted gruffly, his face kinder than ever and more like a frog's.

For a moment Erin compared the pear-shaped body with Jesse's broad shoulders, smooth, wide chest and slim hips. She shook her head blindly. It would not do to think of what she must inevitably regret. She must thank God he'd made her so favourable in Kerruish's eyes. They said he'd do better with his mines than with his boats. He'd be swimming in gold sovereigns one day.

She pressed his hand and let it go. Sebastian was curled against her body. He still insisted on feeding at her breast for all he was past the age for it. Time to break him of the habit before she came to this house for good.

* * *

'You were disturbed above Bay Stacka by the deceased Luke Karran,' Captain Jayce suggested softly.

'No.' Jesse refuted stolidly. 'I never saw Luke on the cliff.'

'In all the years you lived in such close proximity and so near to the Chasms, you *never* saw Karran on the cliff path?'

'Well—I wouldn't say never—'

'But you *have* just said it,' Jayce reminded the prisoner smoothly.

'I didn't mean—'

'What *did* you mean, then?' Jayce slapped his leather boot with the small switch he habitually carried. The sound echoed in the narrow dark chamber. Damp crept out of the stones.

'I meant I didn't see him the night he didn't return home.'

'You hated the dead man, didn't you?'

Jesse swallowed. 'You couldn't be expected to like someone who got your niece with child and never did anything to help afterwards, except deny it.'

'You're sure it was Karran?'

'You've only to look at the little girl. Luke all over.'

'So you admit you had a strong grudge against Karran.'

'Not strong enough to want to kill him. Anyway, Clemence was all right by then because Hugh Conroy took both her and the child— A good man, Hugh—'

'But you saw Luke Karran every day, going or coming from his work and you didn't forget that he'd enjoyed your niece and shirked his responsibilities. You were in the habit of going to the cliff to signal to William Ellis. I say that you met Karran that evening, you had words and fought, killing him. Then you had to dispose of the tell-tale body and not far away was a perfect hiding-place. Except that the cleft you chose had an inconvenient ledge some thirty feet down. If the body had bounced off it would have plunged another hundred and seventy feet and no one would ever have known. That was the way of it, wasn't it, Kinrade?'

'No. No!!'

'No use to shout, Kinrade. It won't add to your sentence because smuggling's a topping offence so you might as well confess and the case can be closed. Nice and tidy.'

'If you think I'm going to tidy up a case when I'd nothing to do with Luke's accident, you're mistaken, Captain Jayce!'

The switch struck the thick leather boot with a vicious crack. 'You're annoyed because I told you your wife had every prospect of becoming a successful street-walker. I suspect you've thought of that for yourself. She'll make a fortune—'

'You pig!' Jesse launched himself towards the captain, taunted beyond endurance. The switch cracked across his cheek, then his shoulder. Stumbling, Jesse collapsed with a pain that set him writhing on the floor, fingers tearing at the flagstones.

'Resisting arrest. Again!' Jayce mocked hatefully and walked away.

The door clanged shut.

*　*　*

Clemence came to see him, her face tormented as she took in the dark surroundings and the dim chill of the place.

'You're hurt.' She touched his cut cheek and swollen eye.

'I fell.'

'There's something for your supper. I don't suppose you'll have much worth eating.'

'Not much.'

'Why did you keep on with Ellis?' She looked like an angel in the diffused light that crept through the small window, Jesse thought, so fair and curiously pure.

'For Erin's sake. It was all I could do for her. She needed something—extra.'

'He's to be hanged.' Clemence said with difficulty. 'But he was the ringleader. They won't—?'

Jesse laughed unconvincingly and opened the parcel of cheese and oatbread and the pat of butter that would normally have gone to market. ' 'Twill take a lot to kill me off. Where's Erin? When they said—a female visitor—I must admit, I did hope.'

'Looking for work. The Master's to redeem the cottage. They say a cousin of his is to take over the croft.'

'Damnation!' Jesse struck the wall with his bunched fist and seemed not to see the blood that appeared on his knuckles. 'I thought the Excise would be so busy

145

with *Glass Lady* they'd not bother with Stacka Bay. I could have sent all that stuff to the sea bed.'

'Is Erin really worth it?' Clemence said bitterly, thinking of the rumours that Erin was to shift to Castletown. In Barney Kerruish's employ.

'You'll not speak so of my wife,' Jesse cried out, 'and you a bastard's mother!'

Clemence, stung, retorted, 'And what if I said she'd already found a post? With Mr. Kerruish of the shipyard?'

There was a silence that seemed to last forever. Before her eyes, Jesse shrank into himself.

'What's that you say?' he said at last, his voice almost a whisper. The past rushed back.

'Well, she has the children and Master wants the roof from over her head. Hugh and I haven't the room and where's the alternative?'

'Damn Kerruish and his money! I know what that means. Even if they do let me out, she'll never come back. But whatever Jayce says, the shipmaster's better than the streets of Castletown.'

'What are you talking about?'

'Nothing that need concern you, my bonny lass. How's Hugh? And Karran and little Joseph?'

'Well enough.'

'And the child you carry?'

Clemence shrugged. 'What with all the worry—I've not felt so well. But it'll pass. Everything passes, Uncle Jesse. You must never give up hope.'

Jesse did not answer. He was seeing Erin at the shipmaster's house. The frog could still turn into the fairy prince. The thought was more bitter than gall. His Erin—

'I must go.'

'Thank you for coming, but don't come again. Think of the baby. It's bad for you.'

'I'm sorry for what I said.'

'I am too.'

But their parting was less warm than it should have been. Too much had passed between them.

Jesse pushed aside the gift of food. Dead men did not need it.

* * *

'So,' Captain Jayce said reflectively. 'You remember you *did* meet the deceased Karran above the bay. Quite near the Chasms, in fact.'

'Yes.'

'Not quite the same story as you told me this morning.'

'No.'

'And?' The switch flicked the soft, smooth leather ever so lightly.

'We did have words—'

'I see.' The captain's hand was very still.

'I did resent the way he treated Clemence. She was a good girl.'

'So?'

'After I had killed him, I put him down the cleft. Just to tidy up the records.'

'You could have saved yourself time and injury.'

'This morning I fancied I had something to fight for.'

'What changed your mind?' The Captain was rising, his eyes curious.

'Nothing I want to talk about.'

'You know what this means?'

'It doesn't matter.'

It might have done, the Captain reflected. Some of the deemsters thought that Ellis's head would have served as an example. Jesse's crime was very small in comparison, and a crofter had excuses. But now that murder was added to the rest—

The sound of his departure was like the closing of a tomb.

PART TWO

BEGINNINGS

CHAPTER FIVE

Erin woke up, her heart thudding. The nightmares
did not happen so often now. Barney lay close beside
her, his arm around her waist as though he expected
her to vanish in the night. His body felt soft and
paunchy, not as Jesse's once did. Her blood clamoured
briefly for long past delights. But Jesse was bones in
that felon's grave and it did no good to remember his
touch and the pounding inside her body. Neither must
she dwell on his bruised face and the misery of his last
days.

Clemence had lost her reason when she knew that
Jesse was dead. Erin could hear her screaming now. 'It
was your fault, Erin Doyle! Yours alone. It broke his
heart when he knew you'd gone to that fancy man in
Castletown. I'll never speak to you again and nor will
any child of mine.'

Karran had listened with that dark, scooped-out face
that was all eyes and cheekbone, the antithesis of
Erin's own brood. Boyce, Elizabeth and Sebastian were
the most beautiful children in the Isle of Man. And
Charlotte? Charlotte was Erin's one mistake. She had
willed Barney's child to take after her but that insistence hadn't worked. Charlotte was plain as a pikestaff
and had no spirit. Not like Boyce and the two Kinrades.

Barney shifted in his sleep and twined his fingers in
Erin's long hair. The image of Jesse receded and she
thought of her life as Mrs. Kerruish. A huge bed with

scented sheets and big, comfortable pillows. Velvet curtains and sofas, fine china and silver. A cupboard full of bed-linen and napery. Luxurious towels and perfumed soap. Wines and tea and good cuts of meat from the butcher. Oranges and grapes, boxes of exotic fruits. And all because she had been Barney's dream, the one weakness in an otherwise shrewd and capable brain. To him she was perfect, a vision he had clung to throughout the years of her marriage to Jesse. He'd not looked at another woman.

The shadow of Jesse's cell returned to lie over her self-satisfaction. If it had not been for her constant demands, Jesse would have given up the contraband once he had responsibilities. His hard, vigorous body dangling from a rope— She shivered.

'Awake, my love?' Barney's soft, excited whisper exorcised the guilt and the horror. But not the momentary distaste for her husband's touch.

She stretched, mock-sleepily. 'M'm.'

'I'm glad you are.' The plump hand dragged the folds of the expensive night-gown up to her thighs. It was hard now for Erin to remember their wedding-night, Barney undressing behind a screen and emerging nervously in a brocade houserobe that only accentuated the tendency to amplitude. She had to teach him everything. He was green as a schoolboy and as grateful. But he'd been a receptive pupil.

She wished he were not so long about the business but there was always a reward at the end of it. It would be foolish to discourage him when her life was just as she had once envisaged it. If only it were Jesse who was with her, raising her to peaks she had half-forgotten and would never reach again.

Erin made the appropriate sounds and Barney was satisfied. She had made him feel no end of a buck. He enjoyed the sensation of being Master.

She endured his soft, damp kiss. There would be time for a bath as soon as he left her. It would all be washed away. And he was not to know that there would never be a son to inherit what he left. After

Charlotte she would never risk having a boy so plain and disappointing. Mistress Payne knew what would keep her free of child-bearing. Camomile and ergot and the like.

'I love you,' Barney said close to her ear.

'And I you,' she replied and stifled the yawn that threatened to engulf her.

It was Sebastian who wanted to claim all of her attention once Barney had gone to the boatyard, but it was Boyce she truly loved. He had been the result of her brief liaison with Dermot O'Neill. Remembering his father's blistering comment on their star-crossed idyll, she still reacted angrily. 'She's the leavings of a dung-heap, Dermot, and never forget it. It's Maureen Kennedy you knew you were to wed and you jeopardise the love of a decent girl like that, and all those expectations, to roll in the hay with the likes of that tinker trash! I'll take the horsewhip to you if you as much as look at the bitch in future. Just tell me what you intend, here and now.'

Dermot had chosen his clean-living and remunerative Maureen with her rich father and good connections, and, when his own choleric and bigoted father died, there'd be his heritage too. If she'd known how to write she'd have told Dermot about Boyce but she could manage no more than a cross. Boyce looked no different from Jesse's two, but the good blood of Ireland ran in his veins. Boyce had class and a grandfather with a title. A pity there would never be proof of his ancestry. He looked only like his mother. But, she hugged the knowledge to herself. Her boy could have been Sir Boyce O'Neill of Killanne if his father hadn't been so spineless.

Smiling, her luxuriant hair loose and beautiful, the green silk houserobe echoing the colour of her eyes, Erin gathered her children around her. Only Charlotte, brown and alien, remained aloof.

* * *

Clemence, standing behind the Conroy stall with Karran at her side, saw the beauteous Mistress Kerruish pass by, a little gaggle of well-dressed redheaded children in her wake. She had not changed. Slightly more voluptuous perhaps, but her red and white colouring was just as heart-stopping. Only the mousy little Kerruish girl lagged behind. It was lucky she was not like Barney, but took after her paternal grandfather. Charlotte would still have a hard time keeping up with those glorious stepbrothers and sister.

Erin's ear-bobs and rings glittered in the sunlight and it was all Clemence could do to restrain herself from shouting abuse like a fishwife. She looked away.

'They're my cousins, aren't they,' Karran said.

'Half-cousins.'

'Why don't we ever speak to them?'

'Because Mrs. Kerruish's selfishness caused my uncle's death. He stole to give her pretty, useless things and he was found out. She never spoke up for him. Women can live perfectly easily without trinkets.'

'I remember Uncle Jesse. At least, I think I do.'

'Then you know what I mean.'

'But *they* didn't harm him. Not Mrs. Kerruish's children.'

'Why do you want to speak to them! You have Joseph and Dinah.'

'They look—interesting.'

'They'll be like their precious mother! Greedy and grasping! Oh, yes, Mistress Quayle, what would you like today? . . . Yes, I have Croggan cheese and honey. Karran! Get out a whole cheese, and was it two or three pots of honey, ma'am?'

Karran squinted into the bright sunlight. The Kerruishes were still in sight, tall and splendid, the light turning their hair to orange splendour. All but the littlest. She looked lonely.

Karran, as she bent to take out the largest of the cheeses, wondered if the flamboyant offspring of her mother's mortal enemy knew that she was closely related to them. The eldest boy looked as if he might be fun, even if Miss Elizabeth was haughty and too aware of her own importance. They'd taken Mr. Kerruish's name, almost as if Mistress Erin was ashamed of her previous life and wanted to forget Uncle Jesse entirely. Master Sebastian was a bit of a cry-baby but he always had been, even as an infant. Karran was downright sorry for Charlotte. Poor little mouse.

Later, Clemence sent Karran off for some sweetmeats to take back for Joseph and Dinah.

She could not believe it when Captain Jayce stopped for a cheese and a fowl.

'I think I'd prefer not to serve you,' she told him, white-faced and proud.

'You have goods to sell. You can't refuse,' he answered curtly. 'I could revoke your license.'

'After what you did to my uncle? To hang him for so little? I don't know how you have the cheek.'

'So little? He was a murderer by his own confession.'

'That's a lie! He'd never hurt a fly.' Clemence stared at Jayce's tall, intimidating figure, the cold, well-chiselled features. Why had he come today when she was at last learning to forget? He usually bought from one of the other stalls and she affected not to see him, in spite of her hatred.

'There might have been leniency if he had not told me he killed Luke Karran.'

The cheeses and the honey pots dimmed and shivered. Clemence was on the slope of Slieu Whallian, on the rim of the Chasms, and Luke was shouting lies. Falling—

Johanne had said all those that Clemence loved came to bad ends. Their dead faces mocked her. Lily's, Joseph's, Sammy's. Luke's—Jesse's—How many more? Not that there were many she truly loved. Deborah, perhaps.

Jesse couldn't have confessed.

'No,' she whispered. 'He couldn't have told you that. Why didn't I know?'

155

'Your husband knew. Perhaps he thought you'd be too upset.'

That must have been when she miscarried. She'd been very ill. But Hugh had been told why Jesse must hang and he'd not explained matters to the captain or parish constable.

'Why did you stop here today?' Her voice was dry as onion skins.

'Because your cheese looked better than anyone else's.' The answer was so simple that she could have laughed and gone on laughing. If the cheese had not been so inviting she'd have gone on thinking it was Erin's fault that Jesse died. But it was her fault. Hers and Hugh's. She wondered how she could live with the knowledge.

* * *

All the way home, Clemence brooded about the revelation. Karran was astride Fiddler, her black hair tossed backwards to show all the dark, sulky planes of her face. She was Luke inside a woman's body. Thank God Johanne and Aggie had gone before Jesse's confession. Too many of their predictions had come true. The baby lost, cattle and crops dying.

The sledge jolted over a hardened rut and Clemence bit her lip. Blood trickled on to her shawl but she stared unseeingly, trying to unravel the complicated pattern of her life. Because her family drowned she had gone to Jesse, and because he had taken responsibility for her he seemed to sense her participation in Luke's death, a death Luke had brought on himself. Because Jesse had died, needlessly, Erin had achieved her objective in bettering herself. None of it made sense. But Hugh should have told her. If they'd gone to Captain Jayce together with their story, things would never have taken that terrible turn. She'd not known Hugh could be so secretive.

Karran was whistling as she guided horse and sledge. She was more like an errand boy than a girl.

156

"The Spanish Lady". That was a favourite of Jesse's and Clemence could not bear the sound. Her frayed nerves snapped.

'Stop that!' Clemence shouted. 'Stop it, do you hear? If it hadn't been for you, none of it would have happened. It's all your fault.'

Luke's black eyes stared down at her.

'Don't look at me! Look at the path ahead, you careless girl. Haven't you been responsible for enough? I wish you'd never been born.'

Karran, seeing the demented look that blotted out her mother's fragile prettiness, was suddenly afraid. She dug her knees into Fiddler's flanks so that he galloped along the track, rocking the sledge from side to side. Behind her, Clemence was muttering to herself. Once she laughed very softly, then resumed the harsh whispering that Karran could not quite hear because of the grating of the runners and the noise of hooves. They were going through the wood now and the trees soared in a dim confusion of green and shadowy mauve. Forests were like churches, still and holy.

It was a terrible thing to know that your own mother wished you dead. Not being born at all, did that make one dead? She wanted to drown out that vision of nothingness and began to whistle again. The soft, eerie notes of "The Spanish Lady" began to haunt the misty recesses of copse and spinney.

Joseph and little Dinah came out at the rattle of the sledge up the incline towards the cottage. Hugh followed them, his face tired from his day's work. The children went to Fiddler, patting him and pushing pieces of carrot under his mouth.

'What is it?' Hugh asked, instantly aware of some change in his wife.

'Don't you know?' she said harshly and dabbed at the blood on her mouth.

'How can I unless you tell me? Karran, will you take Joseph and Dinah in and see to their tea? Your mother and I must talk.'

Over her shoulder, Karran saw Clemence stand up and Hugh take her arm. Clemence freed herself. She looked ghastly, so pale and old as to be almost a stranger. As they moved away Karran wanted to go after them, longing to know the reason for her mother's outburst. She *must* know.

Hurriedly, she sat the children at table with mugs of buttermilk and a piece of oatbread, then ran along the path her parents had taken. They were in the copse and Karran caught glimpses of Clemence's blue gown and ashy coloured hair. Now they had stopped and the child crept as close as she could, screening herself with a holly bush that bulked conveniently near.

'You were always a coward, Hugh,' Clemence said in a stony voice.

'I can't agree.' Hugh was stiff with hurt. 'I didn't run away *that* night.'

'Better perhaps if you had.'

'You can't have it both ways.'

Clemence did not answer.

'I went to see Jesse. He told me that if I involved you and me, they'd hang all three of us. They'd assume that he'd been there as well as us. Whatever reason he had for taking the blame on himself—and no one can know that now—Jayce would never have let Jesse go. He'd had his suspicions about him and Luke for a long time and he's not a man who changes his opinions. Should I have made an orphan out of Joseph and sent my mother early to her grave, aye, and as good as murdered you, all for an accident? And you'd had enough to bear, losing the child and lying between life and death of the fever. You would have me a monster! It was plain they had their hooks in Jesse for both smuggling and for Luke. And Ellis was hanged— Jesse would have been treated the same. It made no difference.'

'You should have tried—'

'If anything would have been bettered, do you think I wouldn't! Jayce was determined to get a confession to tidy up his records. Nothing was made public. In fact he warned me not to spread the story around. A death-bed confession that improved the Captain's expectations. I wasn't going to see you die for anything so useless. I love you—'

'But I don't love you and never have.' How cruel she was!

'Clemence—'

'I should have brought Karran up myself instead of letting you play benefactor.'

'I've never held it against the child that she was Luke's. I've treated her just like the others.'

'But she *isn't* like them. She's Luke's bastard and full of his badness and wickedness.'

'At least that's a change from always insisting everything bad stems from *you*. All that nonsense about some shadow that destroys those you love. You've ruined both our lives for holding to that old badness of Johanne's.'

'I—I wonder where she is now?'

'Be thankful you don't know.'

'I have the strangest feeling she's—dead, but still watching. Like Luke did on our wedding-night. She's died in some ditch like a tinker. I feel her. See her—'

'Stop that, Clemence, d'you hear?'

'I *am* wicked.'

Hugh relented. 'You mustn't blame yourself.'

Karran could not bear to hear the rest of Hugh's conciliatory speech. Things that had been mysteries were now as clear as glass. She had bad blood in her. There had been that terrifying woman who had told her she was her grandmother and then had gone away. The thoughts went crashing through her mind just as her heedless feet crushed the sticks and bracken. Dead heather roots lay twisted like snakes, scratching at her bare ankles. She did not cry out in spite of the pain.

She did not stop until she was tired. Panting and distressed, she leaned against a tree, the rough bark biting into her forehead. A wren flew up into a high branch. Poor wren. It would be hunted in December and put into a casket with a beribboned cushion inside. Streamers would flutter gaily as it was carried from house to cottage, shiny with evergreen, everything pretty except the wren with its limp neck and dull eyes. They'd sing

'We'll away to the wood says Robin to Bobbin,
We'll away to the wood says Dickon to Robin,
We'll away to the wood says Jack o' the land,
We'll away to the wood says everyone.'

Karran cried out at the wren, sending it higher still. 'Don't trust anyone!' she shouted. 'There's no one to trust! No one's what they seem.'

They'd have discovered by now that she had gone but she might as well be hung for a sheep as for a lamb. Wishing that she hadn't thought about hanging, she made her way past the Chasms. There was a big house above Perwick Bay she'd like to see at closer quarters.

Ravensdowne.

There were new people at the house. The Mangolds had left last winter to live in the South of France because of Tom's rheumatics, and Ravensdowne had stayed empty for a time while a few couples had come from the mainland to inspect the isolated property, which had proved too large and remote for most. It had a beautiful position on the edge of the cliff, overlooking the small bay where the Shag Rock protruded from the sea and was frequented by cormorants.

Karran liked cormorants. They reminded her of black swans except that they were more sinuous and graceful. There was a dark magic about them.

The deep cliff-top lane dipped and she could see the glen, smoky dim, with the sound of water through it. 'We'll away to the wood says Jack o' the land.'

The memory of the jingle that accompanied the custom of hunting the wren made Karran unhappy. She did not like to think of anything small and helpless dying to provide amusement, and a wren was smaller and more inoffensive than most.

There was a cottage in the wood, right on the edge where it, also, looked across the sea. It was inhabited occasionally, belonging as it did to a family who had gone to live in Cumbria but had not relinquished the Manx tholtan that still stood, strong and weather-proof. Karran, looking in through the small window, saw the light strike a hearth in which the ashes still remained and a table on which crocks stood unwashed as if the occupant had just gone out.

Something moved across the floor and she sprang back in revulsion. Rats, most probably, though she wouldn't have objected to mice. She rather liked those. The gate stood half-open as though someone might come back at any moment.

She went on, aware that she was hungry and that it was getting very dark. She had been too absorbed in the shocking events of the day to notice the approach of the storm.

Karran saw Ravensdowne suddenly, black against a purplish sky, the sea whipped up into white horses. Her heart swelled at the awe and strangeness of the scene. Behind her was the tholtan, tiny and secretive, before her the mansion on the cliff, so different and yet so oddly bound together. And then the sky was cracked apart with vicious lightning and a series of thunder crashes that beat against her eardrums with an almost physical violence. Yet part of her exulted in the unleashed fury of the elements and the warm rain that lashed her from head to foot so that her hair was flattened to her head and her clothes to her body.

Gasping, she rushed for shelter but the ground outside the gates of the big house was devoid of trees or bushes. Only inside the gardens would she find some niche or cranny where she could escape the worst of the rough weather. Dashing under the shadow of two glistening lions that topped the granite gateposts, she ran down the drive, her gaze going from side to side in search of a haven.

The rain and thunder drowned the sound of hooves behind her and it was only when the horseman was almost upon her that she whirled in shocked disbelief, seeing only a giant silhouette against the plum-dark sky. She flung herself aside just in time. A man shouted but in throwing herself towards the trees, her head had struck one of the trunks. The noise of the storm was lost in a black and silent river.

* * *

Karran woke to the crackle of a fire and the whisper of rain across a window-pane. Her head, which was against a large, lavender-scented pillow, hurt a good deal. The shapes and colours of the room were oddly blurred.

Someone placed a wet cloth across her brow. 'Concussion, the surgeon says,' a voice said quietly. 'She was lucky not to kill herself. What was she doing there? If it hadn't been for that bend in the drive I'd have seen her sooner. The darkness and the storm didn't help.'

'She was trespassing.' It was a woman's voice this time, or Karran thought it was. There was a clipped hardness about it that reminded the girl of watching the smith shoe a horse. The tap, tap, bang of his hammer on the smoking redness. The stink of horn—

'Wouldn't you, with the sky full of thunder? And the lightning was bad.'

'A tinkerish-looking creature. More like a boy than a girl.' A queer satisfaction now permeated that oddly masculine voice. But the light was too bright to see.

'Really, Emily—'

'We'd best count all the spoons if you intend to keep her here.'

'Of course I intend to let her stay. Until she's fit to go—'

'She could have wandered from some encampment. She was probably stealing your rabbits and hens' eggs. Poaching. You always were a Sir Galahad, though, my

162

dear, weren't you. That's how we came to be here. You thinking a change would do me good. Rescuing me from my doldrums in London.' The accompanying laughter was sharp.

'I've never enjoyed looking upon others' unhappiness.'

'You know nothing about that.'

'Only because you've always refused to confide in me. It seems it had something to do with that chambermaid who ran away. Kate—'

'Kate?' The voice had changed, was filled with caution, then a repressed anger that threatened to overcome the original emotion. 'She was rude and disobedient and what does she matter so long afterwards. It's this girl who's the problem. Someone must be worrying about her whereabouts, I suppose.'

No one would be fretting, Karran thought with unaccustomed bitterness. Her mother wished she'd never been born and had told Hugh—she could never think of him as her father again—that she was as full of wickedness as her real father.

'Don't pity yourself!' a small voice inside Karran said contemptuously. 'You're alive, aren't you? You must shape your own destiny if others are not disposed to care.'

She fell asleep listening to that voice.

A man was staring down at her when she awoke the second time. He was tall and weather-beaten and there were tiny, pale creases at the corners of his eyes as if he spent a good deal of time out in the sunlight. His hair was swept back in crisp wings that were more grey than brown. He was subtly different from the men with whom she had previously associated. Karran thought she liked the suggestion of distinction. The stranger was more handsome than many a man less than half his age.

'Well,' he said, as her eyes opened more fully. 'I must say you've given us the fright of our lives. What possessed you to caper about in the middle of the drive in all that downpour?'

'I wanted shelter.'

'Where were you bound for?'

'Nowhere in particular.'

He frowned, but it was more in perplexity than anger. 'In the middle of a storm?'

'I hadn't noticed that. It was fair when I left home.'

'That must have been hours before.' His strong fingers drummed against the coverlet.

Some instinct made her tell the absolute truth. 'I overheard my parents—well, the two people I'd always thought were my parents—quarrelling. It seems Hugh is only my stepfather and I had a father who was so wicked that my mother told me she wished I'd never been born. I'm a bastard, so she told Hugh.'

There was a silence, then he said, 'So you ran away? I'm sure your mother was under some enormous emotional strain when she divulged all this. Perhaps you should have tried to comfort her. How old are you?'

'Thirteen.'

'Thirteen, and it's the first time she let out the secret. Doesn't that tell you anything?'

'She's turned against me, and Hugh who's always been kind and loving. That's what—'

'Frightened you?'

'Of course not!' Karran sat up against the bed-head but the crushing pain returned. White-faced, she pressed her hands against her temples.

'Lie down,' the stranger said. 'It's far too early to start asserting yourself.'

'It was all over Uncle Jesse—' She slid down again thankfully.

'Jesse Kinrade?'

'That's right. But how did you—?'

'Know? You never buy a house without getting the full story of its past from somebody or other. Kinrade used to bring illegal luxuries to the back door and ended up on a rope for his pains. And his beautiful widow made a very good marriage once the gossip died down. Kerruish, the boat builder and would-be mining magnate. Only the land he acquired was a disappointment and he's on the track of more.'

'I didn't know that. Mama doesn't—care for Erin.' It seemed better than mentioning hatred.

'It's always the same way. The newcomer sees more and finds out more than the native.'

'I meant to come here,' Karran said, emboldened. 'I've always thought this was the finest house on the island. This point of Man, anyway. I've never been further than Douglas or Peel. But it's the way it perches above the cove and the rocks and not another house in sight. Not even the cottage.'

'Ah, the cottage.'

It was plain that the new owner of Ravensdowne did not like the proximity of the old tholtan. Yet, he'd seemed so open-minded in other ways.

'Why don't you like the place?'

'Discerning child. It seems to me to attract vermin and would be better razed to the ground.'

'I wouldn't want to destroy someone else's home. Just because you have lots of money and can buy a house like this one, why should another person's cottage have to be pulled down? You said yourself —no, it was me. It's quite out of sight. You don't even have to think about it.'

'I must let your mother know you're here.' The man dismissed the topic on which they were never likely to agree. 'What's her name? And yours.'

'Clemence Conroy. That's Mother. And I'm Karran. From Croggan.'

'Croggan, eh? Not so far from the Calf.'

'Not far.'

'You have to go back. You do see?'

'Perhaps I do. But I know since yesterday, that Mama doesn't want me.'

'Now, now! She was tired or ill or unhappy.'

'That's when people tell the truth. At other times, they pretend.'

'My dear little philosopher—or should that be cynic?'

'Tell them I can't come till I'm better. My head does hurt.'

He looked at her very kindly and Karran was drawn to him. Impulsively, she clutched at his hand.

'John, dear, why didn't you tell me she was awake?' A woman came into the room. She could have been the man's sister, tall and contained with grey in her abundant hair. Even her searching eyes were grey. But she was not warm as he was.

'Didn't know myself until five minutes ago. Her name's Conroy—'

'Kinrade,' Karran said almost angrily. 'It's Kinrade.'

'Then, did you never wonder—' John asked and shrugged.

'I thought I was born before Hugh and my mother wed. It does happen. I thought Hugh was my father. It's all such a tangle. No one told me. It—confuses me.'

'What *are* you talking about?' the woman enquired with cool amusement.

'It's nothing, Emily. I'll explain later. Would you like something to eat, child?'

'I'm not hungry.' The pain in Karran's head was making her feel sick.

'The doctor will be back. He'll decide what's best,' Emily murmured. 'She's a very handsome child. Such a strong face.' She sounded more alive.

'To match her personality,' John said. 'She's almost painfully truthful.'

'Is truth so hurtful?' the woman called Emily murmured reflectively.

'It can be.'

'She's dark as a gipsy. Do you think it wise, John, to interfere in this business of her forbears? Though, if I'd been her mother, I'd have allowed the girl to take the husband's name.'

'He may not have wanted that. Look, she's practically asleep. We'll talk over a dish of tea. Come, wife.'

Wife, Karran thought drowsily. They had not looked married. But, of course, they were quite old.

*　*　*

It was several days before Karran was taken home.
Her benefactors were John and Emily Howard from
London. She had asked John, who was a retired
businessman, why they should want to come from
such a lively and interesting city to a house on a cliff
and he'd told her that a tentative week's holiday some
years ago had proved so rewarding that they'd come
several more times and liked Man better and better.
Karran had the impression it was John who became so
besotted.

'It was the contrast from endless streets and smoking chimneys. From eternal noise.'

'But what did you find here?'

'Peace, I suppose. But most of all, the flora and
fauna.'

'Whatever are they?'

'Plants and beasts.'

'Flora and fauna!' Karran laughed and her black eyes
sparkled. 'How quaint!'

'Doesn't it thrill you to know that Bishop Wilson
found a mass of trees thrown down in some immense
southerly gale of long ago and preserved in a bog? And
there's a submerged forest in Poyllvaaish bay. And
there's black horehound and thrift and erica cruci-
ata—'

'Erica what!'

'Cross-leaved heath. There's a clue. Crucifixion and
crosses. And there are water-lilies, ling, ragwort,
foxgloves, honeysuckle, bog-myrtle, hares and rabbits.
They say the Derby family brought over the rabbits but
the hare is a natural. Rats have only just arrived—on a
Russian vessel, the worthies told me. Stoats, seals,
porpoises, bats, but it's the birds I love. In London
there might be sparrows and starlings but here! The
cormorants alone would drive a man mad with
pleasure. Magpies, jackdaws—I saw a field completely
filled with jackdaws the other day. I've a spy glass to

167

train on the cliffs and you'd never believe the things I see— The variety in the gardens—'

'I should like to see them.'

'And so you shall, my dear. Finish up the soup. It will do you good.'

'So, here you are again, John.' Mrs. Howard was there, smiling, but cool as buttermilk.

'Ah, Emily. I thought I must see how Karran improves. I fear she is so greatly better that she'll soon be gone.'

'I don't want to go!'

'Karran—'

'They don't want me and you do. You do, don't you?' Her eyes beseeched his.

'There are things it's wiser not to say. We cannot kidnap you however much a child would liven our home.'

'Couldn't you have any of your own?'

'No,' Emily said, a little tight-lipped. 'But John always wished—' Her knuckles were white.

'Dammit!' John espostulated in rare bad humour. 'There's half the world with an over-abundance and the other half famished.'

'Glut and famine,' Emily echoed, uncharacteristically, Karran thought. She had so many real opinions of her own. So much character.

'The wind's rising,' John said. 'Would you like to see the bay, Karran?'

'Oh, yes! Yes.'

Wrapped in a handsome, quilted robe that was far too large, the girl pressed her nose to the wide glass pane that showed her so much more than the leaded ones at Croggan.

The grey sea was whipped into great white-crested waves that curled and threw up huge pillars of spume to cover Shag Rock and the small promontory that marked the left side of the bay. Then it was as though some giant finger pulled back the sea to leave the black rocks bare, then released the turbulent waters to drown them, over and over, like some inexorable fate.

168

The sound of the ever-encroachng tide echoed in Karran's mind.

Emily had gone about her business and only John was there, safe and sane in a world that had receded except for the mansion above the bay. She loved John.

Karran snuggled down inside the house-robe that obviously belonged to him with its smell of tobacco and pomade, those inkstains on the cuffs.

The sea surged and sent up a white curtain that made her cry out with excitement.

John's arm came around her shoulders. She felt safe. So very safe—

* * *

'So, you're back.' Clemence looked very odd and her eyes were rimmed with fatigue.

'Yes, Mama.'

'You were lucky they were good people, taking you in the way they did.'

'Yes.'

'Why did you do it?'

Karran looked her mother straight in the eye. 'You told me you wished I'd never been born. Then, I heard you say that I was full of my father's badness and wickedness. That I had bad blood in me. I thought you didn't want me.'

'Oh, Karran.'

'You did, though, didn't you, and I know you meant it.'

'I'm sorry but you weren't intended to hear. You eavesdropped and listeners seldom hear good of themselves.'

'There was an old woman in the cottage over there, years ago. She said she was my grandmother.'

'She was a bad woman.' Clemence had turned pale.

'Then she must have been,' Karran taunted. 'It's the sort of grandmother I would have.'

Karran relented when she saw Clemence's distress. She remembered John's words and tried to help her mother but it seemed that Clemence did not want to be helped. And Hugh was constrained, as though he, too, blamed Karran for being her father's child. Who was her father? What was he like? And did Clemence really kill those she loved? How?

She asked Meg Conroy about Luke and Meg was evasive at first, but, seeing how serious the girl was, she told Karran the gist of the story.

'I don't think I would have liked him,' Karran said. 'Wouldn't it be awful if I was like him?'

'You only resemble him in looks.'

'How can you tell?'

'My dear child, I've known you since you were born, just as I've known Clemence. The Karrans ruined that girl between them but they haven't spoiled you. Hugh will make things right. Thinks the world of your mother, he does.'

But Hugh did not make things much better, in spite of his devotion and industry.

The only bright spot in Karran's life was when John Howard rode over from Ravensdowne to invite her for a visit. Joseph was jealous and Clemence disinclined to allow her to go. 'She's useful here, Hugh, and I can do with her help. She'll get ideas—'

'Remember how you used to rail about Erin Doyle when she found *you* indispensable?'

Clemence, flushing, had changed her viewpoint. 'If you promise you won't expect too much of the attention they give you—'

'Oh, I won't, Mama!'

'Then—you can go. But, remember your place. It's their charity, that's all.'

It was wonderful to be back at the mansion. The wind was rattling the windows and the bay was white with spindrift out of which loomed the intimidating blackness of Shag Rock. Inside, in the warmth of John's study, Karran was happy again.

Together, she and John pored over some illustrated books with coloured etchings of wild life and plants. The little black hieroglyphics that were the text fascinated her. 'What's that?' she asked and went on with her questioning until the page was deciphered.

Howard was amazed that she could not read.

'I've never been taught.'

'I can't imagine why you should be surprised,' Emily said. 'What peasant can?'

'But Karran is different. She's intelligent.'

'She could have the brain of an Aristotle and still need tuition. Even if her family had had the means, she'd not have been sent to university or for a Grand Tour. She's a girl, remember?' Emily was faintly acid. She set down the tray of chocolate and cakes.

'You weren't deprived.'

'No, but thousands are, especially girls. Most never realise their potential.' Emily poured out the chocolate and passed a cup to each. 'If I'd had a daughter I'd have seen that she had an equal opportunity.'

'Why don't we give Karran a chance?' John took his cup to the fireplace and straddled the hearth. He looked very tall from this angle and, with his hair drowned in shadow, younger than usual.

'It's what you've wanted to do since you nearly ran her down.' It was almost an accusation.

The rain slapped the big, exposed windows and ran hissing down the slates. John's eyes sparkled with excitement. 'You can't go back today, Karran. No one'd expect it.'

'No,' Karran said slowly and looked across at the book and the delicate illustrations. 'Wouldn't it take a long time to learn? Only a day every week or two?'

'Hugh Conroy seems to me to be a reasonable man. There's his mother who worships that little Dinah and could keep an eye on her. Joseph's getting big enough to accompany his father. It shouldn't be impossible to borrow you for week-ends and then it would be up to you, Karran. Work and there's no limit to what you can learn and the doors that might open for you.'

'She's a handsome girl,' Emily observed. 'If she had knowledge as well as looks—'

Handsome, Karran thought. It was such a masculine

171

adjective. If only someone would call her pretty. She wasn't, of course. Thick black hair and strongly marked features were far more a boy's attributes. Her father, Luke's looks, and those of that terrible gipsy-like woman who had swept up the dirt and the leaves towards Hugh's cottage and had uttered those threats that no one had ever forgotten. It would be good to get away from Croggan, even if her freedom was only confined to Saturday and Sunday.

'I want to do it,' Karran said. 'I want to read more quickly than anyone else has ever done. I *can* do it.'

John laughed and there was a note of challenge in his voice as he said. 'We'll have a bet on it. Emily and I against you reading—and writing a good hand—inside a year.'

'I *will*!'

'Good.'

'You haven't said what she's to get if she succeeds,' Emily pointed out, gathering up the white, fluted cups and saucers. 'It's not a bet otherwise.'

'A trip to Douglas and fifty guineas to spend.'

'John, is that wise?'

'Is what wise? I thought you approved?'

'In principle. It's the sum involved. It could give rise to jealousies. Mistrust.'

'Fifty guineas in the bank, then, for her future. To accrue interest. And a new gown and bonnet and the fallals to go with it.'

'People will talk.'

'Bother people.'

'She'd have done it without anything quite so grandiose.'

'I know. I just think she deserves better than she may get and no one need know about the money, except for Karran.'

'No good will come of it if you leave out her parents. You'll only put off the inquest.'

'Leave it to me, Emily. It will all come out properly in the end. And now young lady, come here and you will receive your first lesson.'

172

John reached for a sheet of paper and a quill, then wrote two words.

'What are they?' Karran asked.

'The most important words in the world. For you, that is.'

'I don't know what they are but they look—familiar.'

'Your name. Karran Kinrade.'

She stared until the letters seemed to move of their own accord and become an incomprehensible jumble she would never master. But she would master them! She had to. One day they would stand still and the key to their mystery would unlock the door to the future.

* * *

Clemence had balked at first, almost as though she were jealous. But it was she who had turned against Karran. How could she be so divided? It was Hugh who pointed out what John Howard had already seen.

'There's no reason to keep the girl from bettering herself. You didn't care for being Erin Doyle's slave. If I recall, you escaped to Peel, to Deborah's, often enough.'

''Twasn't the same. That's not fair.'

'No?'

'Am I selfish, Hugh?'

'In this instance, yes. It's only for week-ends.'

'They want to keep her for themselves. They've no childer, and he has too little to do since he's given up his money-making.'

'And you'd be happier without her. I'm tired of hearing how it offends you to look at Luke Karran's daughter. It's—dog in the manger to put obstacles in Karran's way.'

'It's—not so simple.'

'Life never is, Clemence.' Hugh's white face showed that he had not forgotten his wife's proclamation that she'd never loved him. That had struck home.

All week, Karran worked harder than usual so that there would be less for Clemence to cope with on her

173

precious two days at the house on the cliff. There must be no obstacle to the delight of learning, or the overcoming of those hieroglyphics. It was the one chance of her life and it was ironic that it had only come about because her mother had revealed her true feelings for the first time.

For a while, Karran had been equally divided. Clemence had been the pivot of her existence, assuming far greater importance than Hugh or their children. Karran was fond of Joseph and Dinah but everyone paled into insignificance against Howard's charm and Emily's steely possessiveness. Mrs. Howard never seemed womanly, just flat-chested and curiously masculine, her tongue quite sharp if she disagreed with her husband's views. It was out of character for women to be so forceful in places like Croggan. Karran sometimes thought it was not so much a child Mrs. Howard desired, but another woman with whom she could experience an affinity. A kindred spirit.

Sometimes Karran had the feeling that Emily disliked her husband, yet who could not be fond of someone like John? Yet, the only real passion that had ever infused Emily's voice was in the way she had spoken about the vanished maid in London. Kate. What had the girl done, or not done? Karran knew she would never understand Emily. Ladies didn't bother about runaway servants. There were always plenty to replace them.

John Howard she understood much better. There was, it was true, an iron fist under the velvet glove where teaching her was concerned, but when they were not in the study with the books and the quills and paper, he could be good company, taking her down to Port St. Mary to the delightful small harbour, or to Port Erin where there was a long stretch of sand where the horses could be allowed their heads. The mounts were not of the hardy Manx stock like Fiddler who had come to Clemence on Jesse's death, but pure-blood aristocratic mares and stallions. Karran could scarcely believe the change in her life.

Emily gave her a riding-habit for Christmas and had made her try it on in her own boudoir, which was very plain and simple in contrast to the guest rooms. She had lingered over patting and smoothing the garments over Karran's slim, boyish body until the girl was uncomfortable. Yet she wanted the dark, severe clothes and could not rebuff John's wife, however much she disliked the unnecessarily prolonged contact.

John approved of the good line of the habit and the starkly white blouse that went with it. He told Karran the hard hat became her as nothing else did. The boots of polished leather and the black gloves delighted her. 'I mustn't grow too much,' Karran said, aware of both absorbed faces, revelling in her unaccustomed importance.

'You won't,' Emily assured her, grey eyes ranging over the firm, young body. 'I'll be surprised if you put on another inch and that won't make a ha'porth of difference.'

It was hard to be taken home on Sunday and to wake up on a Monday in the cramped surroundings of the cottage. Clemence began to pick on her needlessly. 'Oh, you won't want to work your way here after being spoiled at Perwick.'

'I don't mind.'

'Of course you mind! You're such a lady now!'

'You let me go.'

'And it was a mistake! You look down your nose at us.'

'Mama! I don't.'

'And don't call me that.'

'Then, what am I to call you? Mrs. Conroy? I'm your daughter.'

'Dinah's my daughter.'

'Then where do I belong? Tell me, where?' There was no answer.

It was Joseph who came running into the poky living-room one Thursday afternoon, almost oversetting the spinning-wheel.

'Mama!'

'What is it?' Clemence, her face pale in the dimness, the light catching her whitish hair, looked a creature of moonbeams and cobwebs.

'There's a woman at the door of the tholtan. The one nobody's lived in before.'

There was only one derelict cottage and that was the Karrans'. Joseph could not remember Johanne. He'd not make up such a story.

'She's come back,' Clemence whispered and pressed a hand to her breast.

'How can she hurt us?' Karran asked, then recalled the dust cloud and the leaves spinning, the voice that cursed everything but herself.

'Not you, you devil's creature,' her mother said and grabbed Joseph to her. 'Only us.' She was ashen.

There was the sound of twigs brushing the mud of the path, a woman's voice muttering. Clemence gave a cry and clutched at her heart. Joseph, released, staggered against the wall, his face twisted with fear.

Karran opened the door and stood with her back to it.

'I curse everything within,' Aggie Karran said in a queer, sing-song voice. 'Except you, niece. 'Twas my mother's dying wish. The witch's curse.'

'Go away.'

'I'm home,' Aggie told her, looking crazier than ever. Birds could have nested in her hair and her clothes were rags. 'Look out for yourself, Clemence Conroy. Murderess!'

Joseph gave a little scream. There was a faint thud.

'Mama! Oh, Mama! Please, get up.'

Aggie dissolved behind a wall of dust and twigs. Karran ran inside. In the faint pink firelight, she made out Clemence's body lying close to the hearth. Joseph was huddled in the corner, whimpering.

'Mama?' Karran knelt and stared into her mother's face. It was pale as skimmed milk and the little veins in her closed eyelids were blue. Her breast did not move. When Karran lifted her hand it flopped back like a fish.

176

There was no doubt about it. Clemence was dead.

* * *

John Howard rode over when Karran failed to appear and found Hugh distraught and the children tearful. Meg was away at Bessie's for the night and so there was no bulwark.

It was John who arranged for the undertaker to come and for the minister to be told about funeral arrangements. It surprised him that a woman of Clemence's age could simply collapse and die.

''Twas that woman,' Joseph whispered. 'That—witch. Her mother's dead but the badness lives on in her.'

Hugh, white-faced, repudiated the suggestion. 'Clemence must always have had a weakness.'

John, however, persisted in demanding an explanation for Joseph's assertion. Karran told him of the day Johanne had stormed up to the door, cursing everything in sight and out of it. 'And now her daughter is back with a great, dirty gipsy of a husband and two raggedy children who'll make Joseph and Dinah's life a misery. I don't care for myself, they always leave me out of their attacks, but I do care about Hugh and the children.'

'Fear has always been the most potent, if primitive, weapon,' John said soberly. 'There's no way in which the family can be got rid of?'

'It's Johanne's cottage. No one's claimed it since she went. It wasn't worth the trouble, and now that hulking husband of Aggie's is becoming useful to the Master for very little payment. He won't turn them out. You should see Boswell! Seven feet tall and hairy as the devil.'

'Something will have to be done,' John told her. 'This intimidation mustn't go on.'

'I can't come to Ravensdowne meanwhile,' Karran said, fighting back misery. 'But you know it's not

177

because I don't want to. Only, how could I leave them?'

'How, indeed. We'll think of something.'

But it was Hugh who thought about the future and removing his beloved children from the harm he feared would come upon them as it had to poor Clemence.

'We'll emigrate,' he told a silent Karran. 'Go to the Americas. There'll be nobody there to put curses on my boy and girl. I've a little put by towards the passage money and there's boats from Douglas. And you'll come too. You're as much my daughter as Dinah—'

'You want *me* to go to New York?'

'Why not? You're Clemence's flesh and blood. You don't want to be left cheek by jowl with Aggie and her brood, do you? She'll have dozens, all as bad as herself.'

'No. But—America!'

'It's a rare opportunity, lass.'

'I love—Man.'

'You want betterment. You'll get it there. Everyone gets on in America.'

'Let me think,' Karran said desperately.

'Not for too long, lass.'

She went to Meg who knew everything about her and who advised her to do as Hugh suggested. Clemence's early death had shocked the Conroys out of complacency. They'd rather have their son and grandchildren alive on the other side of the Atlantic than buried in Croggan.

'But, the Howards!'

'They'll not stay here for ever,' Meg said. 'Those sort of folks seldom do. There'll be a bad winter or it'll be inconvenient for their friends from London to travel so far. They'll go and you'll be forgotten. You're a novelty and that Mrs. Howard is bored. Hugh'll never let you down. To tell the truth, my Jim and me, we're thinking of going too, so you'd have to come, then, wouldn't you. I'm just waiting for Jim to decide one way or the

178

other— Where are you off to, lass? Karran! Come back!'

Karran ran as she had done that day of the storm, almost without motive. The wood drowned her in shade, whispering and sighing, beautiful beyond words. Where the track divided, she was torn two ways. Spanish Head called her, reminding her of summer with the bees humming around the thrift and gorse and the Sugar Loaf standing out of the water like an old woman with a heavy load. But the other path led to Perwick and John Howard. He would know what was best. Or were he and Emily playing with her and treating her merely as a diversion? A house on a cliff with no others close by could be a lonely place.

The path by the Chasms had never seemed so long, nor the glen so dark and murmurous.

Karran stopped suddenly, her heart bumping in her breast. The cottage door stood open and a trickle of blue smoke drifted from the chimney. A woman appeared in the gap and ran, laughing, round the side of the house. She was fair and pretty, not at all the sort of person one would associate with such a modest dwelling. The gown she wore looked expensive and her hands were snowy white, her hair curled fashionably.

Karran was immediately aware of her own hands, brown and calloused, abused by all manner of field and household chores. Instinctively, she hid them behind her back, just as a young man came out, obviously in pursuit of the fleeing lady. He halted at the sight of Karran and she regretted the faded red jacket and old green kirtle, both reach-me-downs from Erin's day and saved frugally as everything was at Croggan, whether or not it fitted.

The man was attractive in an understated way. He had a thinnish face made interesting by deep, smooth eyelids that hooded his eyes most effectively. The short, straight nose was blunt-ended as were his lips. His cheekbones stood out prominently, giving him a hungry look. Karran had always disliked full faces. Something in her responded.

'What are you selling?' he shouted. 'Clothes-pegs? Or is it heather?'

Karran scowled.

The man laughed. 'Lost your tongue, gipsy? There you are, then.' And he tossed a silver coin towards her. 'It'd be bad luck not to appease you.' Then he crashed his way past the overgrown wall and the lowermost branches of the copse that encroached upon the neglected cottage and was lost to view almost immediately.

She stared at the shilling. It seemed faintly ridiculous that, just as she was seeking safety for her family from the malevolence of her father's kin, a stranger should counteract the ill-fortune she might bring. The world was, briefly, incomprehensible. Then she heard the girl shrieking behind the tholtan and pictured the two strangers together. The silence that ensued told her they were in one another's arms and she kicked away the coin in a revulsion she could not explain.

All the way down the drive to Ravensdowne, she saw the thin, clever face that mocked her.

The Howards received her with their usual appearance of pleasure. While they all sipped chocolate, she told them of the Conroy's decision to leave the island.

'America.' Emily could not conceal her amazement and chagrin. 'And just as we were beginning to know you.'

'You want to go?' John barked, roused to anger.

'Go?' Karran's fingers worked against the faded red that became her better than she realised. 'No. That's why I came here. But they'd not leave me behind at my age and the Master'd want the cottage. Where could I go?'

'Here,' John said with asperity. 'Where else?'

'It was—only Saturdays and Sundays. The arrangement—'

'Now it will be every day.' Howard paced the room. 'They may not let me.'

'They will when I offer to help pay the passages.'

'You want me—so much?' Karran was humbled.

'Didn't you know that?'

Meg had been wrong and so had Clemence. Howard had never looked on her as a temporary easement of country boredom. She was needed.

Karran looked at Emily but encountered only the grey shutters of her eyes made blind by the light from the window.

'And you, Mrs. Howard?'

'Oh, we both want you. In our different ways.'

'I can be made your legal guardian,' Howard told Karran. 'I doubt if Conroy will object. It's not as if he's your father.'

It wasn't true, Karran thought, numbed. Here, always. Always—

'Make him agree. Oh, please—' To remain here, within reach of all she loved, Spanish Head, the Sugar Loaf, Stacka Bay. Even the Chasms with their dizzying perch above the sea. The Calf and Kitterland— Port St. Mary— The cathedral-like woods—

'You want to stay that much?'

'Yes.'

'I'll go over now on the Major and talk to Conroy.'

'But you won't let him think—'

'Think what?'

'That you are buying me? Hugh wouldn't like that.'

'You see, Emily? She's as sensitive as even you could wish. That's the nub of the matter. Don't you worry, Karran. I'll be discreet.'

She went outside with him and watched him ride off, waving to her excitedly as if this was his most important mission. It wasn't any transitory affection he had for her. Karran was suddenly sure of that.

But, Emily. What did she really think? It was something Karran might never know.

CHAPTER SIX

Barney had acquired the lease of the Abraham mine some years before and a new shaft had been sunk in the following spring. He and Erin had made such plans for the find they had not made. The copper had run out with disheartening swiftness and he had made the most of a boom in boat-building to compensate for his losses.

Perhaps the name of the mine was to blame. True, it had been so called to commemorate Wolfe's victory at the Heights, but mines and potholes were queer places, defying nature, and sometimes a change could bring back the luck.

The lease was due to expire within months and the Duke was unlikely to renew it with no recompense in sight. Barney had not managed to retain the best workers, who, after all, had to eat with the rest of them. His Master Joiner had defected to Glen Chass, as had his Master of Lead and the more promising apprentices.

The farmers' sons went back to their fathers' lands and the Irish moved on, tinkering to keep alive, and stealing the Duke's game. He'd be pleased that they were re-employed.

One of the reasons the work force had moved on was that Barney had built only a token number of miners' dwellings. Once the lease was given up or taken away, the miners' rows belonged to the Duke, so a mine-owner must be very sure it was worth his while to build them in the first place.

Barney thought it over most carefully. There was always the shipyard but that could never be expanded, not in Castletown with Quayle's taking up much of the space available, and Quayle was a good boat builder. One only needed to look at his *Peggy* as she went about her business, as stout and dependable a craft as anyone would wish to see. It would be pointless to flex his muscles in Castletown. And there was an excitement in probing the unknown bowels of the earth for something one could only guess at. He must try to woo fate. Then he'd take on more men and start afresh. It would be a challenge.

He and Erin rode over to Foxdale on her birthday and Barney flung a bottle of champagne down the almost defunct shaft, saying 'I name you Erin after my lovely wife.'

Her green eyes glittering like the shards of broken glass, Erin had seized hold of him, uncharacteristically moved by the romantic gesture.

It had ended equally surprisingly by Barney tossing her down on a patch of moorland and lifting her skirts while Erin responded to him for the first time. She could not decide if it was due to the novelty of being tumbled in the open air by a man who was normally conventional, but she was amused and warmed in turns all the way back to the inn from which they'd started.

Next month, the shaft was re-opened and some weeks later, Norton, the overseer, was knocking on Kerruish's door to tell him they had made an encouraging find.

'I said you'd bring me fortune, lass,' Barney cried delightedly and filled Erin's champagne glass to the brim. 'We'll need more miners again at this rate *and* more cottages.'

'Won't that take time?'

'They'll live rough at first. Some huts and tents. But I've an interest in Shanks' building and the miners' row won't present much of a problem. It's the only way to hang on to the men. Once you've given them a proper roof over their heads and they bring wives and make children, they'll think twice before moving.'

'In other words, you have the whip hand, Barney.' Erin sounded pleased.

'Oh, I shan't brandish the big stick too much. Ogres don't arouse the championship I need to make this new venture a success.'

'But you don't want over-familiarity.' Erin was learning to speak as became a woman of importance. She had learnt to drop the Irish "me" and substitute "my" some time ago. The delightful lilt was all that remained of Erin Doyle.

'Decidedly not, my dear,' Barney agreed. 'But there's a state half-way that makes for good relations. Isn't that so, Norton.'

'Yes, Mr. Kerruish.' Norton, dizzy with champagne and relief that he was still in work, would have agreed to anything. But it did make sense, being friends with your employees. In some businesses you never saw your master. Only the overseer who had to fight to retain authority unless he was a kind of martinet. Norton wasn't. This shared responsibility suited him. He was conveniently grateful.

Barney smiled his wide frog smile. Erin thought she had underrated that smile. It had the quality of irradiating happiness. Something in her shied away from the effect of her husband's goodness. It made her feel mean and shabby. The enormity of this confession shocked her into silence. First of all his lovemaking had moved her after years of indifference, and now his smile touched her. She could not understand her own reactions. Long ago she had derided Barney. The frog who would never become a prince. And now, like some wide-eyed innocent, all Barney's hidden qualities were becoming apparent and even she could not help being aware of them.

For the first time in years she no longer thought of Jesse or Dermot O'Neill. She was getting old, Erin decided, half-dismayed, half-accepting. It must be that. She couldn't really— No, the thought was too grotesque—

'The Duke will need to be paid his percentage,' Barney said, leaning back in his chair. Champagne in moderation never altered his capacity for working out the realities of a situation. 'But it was a fair agreement. He'll not lose and neither will I. But it's buying out someone else I have to concentrate on. It's owning the whole that makes a rich man. I need a lead mine, Norton, and I want to know who's in monetary difficulties, who is relinquishing their sett.'

'There's Robertson of Foxdale. I wouldn't have known but for a friendship between his foreman's wife and mine. Women will talk without realising what they divulge. Robertson must sell out, and soon. They say his son has run up huge gambling debts and faces gaol.'

'Thank you, Norton. I'll remember the debt I owe you. You wouldn't know who Robertson's attorneys are, would you?'

'Messrs Grey of Douglas, master.'

'Better still. More champagne, Norton? And you must bring Mistress Norton to supper one evening. Isn't that so, Erin, my dear?'

'Why, yes, Barney. There's nothing I'd like better.' Another thing Erin had accepted quite readily was that business came above all else. To Barney's acumen she owed all her jewels, lace, gowns and luxuries, and, quite belatedly, her happiness.

And then Charlotte pushed her plain little face round the door and spoiled everything.

Barney held out his arms and Erin froze into a statue of white, red and green. He adored that child. She couldn't be jealous? Ridiculously, she was. Sanity returned. Perhaps he did dote on his own flesh and blood, but an unprepossessing child could never compete with a beautiful woman who could give a man her body, her caresses. She was quite safe. Her husband needed her far more than an ugly daughter. The last thing Erin had contemplated was falling in love with Barney but it seemed that she had, or thought she had.

Somewhere the Fates must be laughing.

* * *

The Erin continued to produce the precious lodes. The sinking of the shaft had uncovered various seams that had eluded the previous owners by so little. Barney did not lose sight of the fact that he'd been lucky. Had it been because he'd changed the name of the mine? He would never know for certain. But he was not unaware of Erin's new interest in him.

They had entertained the Nortons who were touchingly gauche and overcome with obligation. Employers rarely, if ever, entertained underlings. Kerruish was something new on the horizon of working men.

Barney had donned a helmet on which a candle burned and descended Robertson's mine that now belonged to him. He was engulfed by darkness, made bearable only by the candlelight that flickered and guttered and showed him eroded stones, shadowed overhangs and clefts, moisture that dripped or flowed in little torrents that presaged trouble. He watched the men who chipped and banged at the rock and made little round holes in the harsh, pale surface.

Now, vaulted tunnels, claustrophobically narrow, reverberated to the tap of hammers. Even the fragile light could not hide the dust that clung to hair and eyelashes. Miners were underpaid, Barney thought, not for the first time. It wasn't the way a mine owner should be thinking. His mind should be on profits, a future for the children, his and Jesse's.

He climbed out of the shaft slowly. He was fond of Charlotte, of course, but he wanted a son, a beautiful boy like Erin. She'd given two such sons to another man and that fascinating minx, Elizabeth. Charlotte had arrived quite soon after their marriage. Then had come years of barrenness and he'd never been able to understand why. Erin still had her courses and they lay together frequently.

The baffling disappointment was forgotten when he emerged into daylight and Norton and the mine carpenter met him at the company office. There were stores to requisition and Barney usually vetted these. There were pick handles, corves and shovels to make from wood fetched from Douglas. Candles. Rope. More ovens for reducing the ore. The carpenter's shop to be extended. The blacksmith's shop to have part of a wall demolished and the lower half of the building taken out at a right angle as it could not, practicably, be lengthened, not with the stream so close. The Powder houses would remain as they were for another six months and, if necessary, two more would be built at the end of the year.

'There's talk of a Man mining company,' Norton said. 'To test the veins running through the district. We should make our own investigations and claims before any nationally-run venture finds them for us.'

'Trials cost money.'

'Aye, but it could gripe a man to find that a bit of extra work could have earned him another seam or two. Maybe a fortune.'

'It's only talk so far, about the Man company.'

'But that usually means it'll come about eventually. They may be slow but they're sure.'

'You're right, of course. But you've enough to do, Norton, looking after Robertson's. Come to think of it, I can't keep calling it that. I could call it the Charlotte, after my lass.'

'A bonny lass,' Norton said dutifully.

'It's Elizabeth you must be meaning,' Barney said bluntly. 'The image of her mother, that pretty little madam. Charlotte's as plain as a pudding. Not fair to her really, not to have taken after Erin. But that's beside the point. Robertson's is no more and this mine is now the Charlotte. Didn't do me any harm to change the name of the other one. We'll need more ground. Who's leased that stretch beyond the stream?'

187

'Reed. From Carlisle. He runs it with a partner, but they've not had much so far.'

'I'd have to drive a fair bargain. Though the Duke will remember how the Erin's prospered. The Dukes have had little luck with most of their mining ventures and you can't blame a man for expecting a return for the use of his land.' As usual, Barney could see and sympathise with his opponents' problems. Yet this never seemed to interfere with his own success.

'And, as I said before, Norton, you've your hands full. What I want is some energetic young man with some special knowledge of geology and engineering to do the trials. If he finds anything, well and good. If not—' Barney shrugged. 'I'm the loser.'

'And where will you find him?'

'Oh, I've had a notion to take a trip to Liverpool for some time. I've contacts there. Come to think of it, my wife would love it. Never managed to take a honeymoon, me with my boats and she with her three rascals, then Charlotte coming so quickly.' Why hadn't there been another? His boy—

'They're growing up now, though, Mr. Kerruish.'

'They most certainly are. Charlotte's nigh on ten so that makes Sebastian twelve or thereabouts, Miss Elizabeth fifteen, and Boyce sixteen. Near enough, anyway.'

'And a credit to you both.'

'Think so, Norton?' Barney brooded for a moment on Sebastian's exaggerated dependence on Erin, on Elizabeth's tantrums and on Boyce's rebellion against his authority. Something would have to be done about those boys, for their own good, particularly Sebastian. It wasn't healthy to be so obsessed with one's mother. He'd been fond enough of his own but he'd kept the affection on a decent plane. Sebastian must go away to school. It would be the making of him.

The only time Sebastian had a separate life from Erin was when he was drawing. If he were allowed paper and pencils or a quill, the boy could retreat inside himself. Some of the sketches had life. Queer subjects

188

they were, though, doors and windows, roofs and chimney pots. Nothing strong and masculine. And Boyce? He was displaying an interest in the Army and he was obviously opposed to going into either of Barney's businesses. Boats made him seasick—so he said—and a mine was claustrophobic. Elizabeth? Another two years and she'd be ripe for marriage. She was so like her mother. His Erin—

He told Erin about his intention to spend a week or two in Liverpool, partly on sight-seeing but mainly to look for a suitable engineer. Barney noticed her look of dismay with a profound pleasure. She thought she was to be left behind and she actually seemed to mind the fact.

He poured our more claret.

'What a lovely colour that is,' Elizabeth said. 'Can I have some? It's pinky-red.'

'It's not a cordial, my love. It's a wine.'

'But I want some!'

'I want seldom gets,' Barney replied with deceptive gentleness. He had a fund of such sayings, a left-over from childhood.

'Papa is perfectly right,' Erin said sharply. 'You'd be tipsy.'

'I'm fifteen, well nearly.' Elizabeth's eyes flashed ominously.

'I think you should go to bed. It might mend your manners.'

'I won't!' The child glared at Barney with a woman's eyes.

'You will,' Erin said loudly. 'Do as you're told. Do as your father says.'

'He isn't my father!'

Erin's voice could be heard all over the house. Elizabeth, taken forcibly upstairs, sobbed hysterically in her own room. The boys sat like handsome judges, one at either side of the table. No one noticed Charlotte, who screwed pieces of bread into small pellets.

'They get more of a handful all the time,' Erin said

189

despairingly. 'They have all they want and yet they are never satisfied.'

'Who says we have?' Boyce, who was allowed claret, was inclined to belligerence.

'I've thought for some time,' Barney told him, 'that you'd benefit from some impartial discipline. I've made up my mind. It's the Army for you, Boyce.'

'It's not your decision!' The handsome face flushed.

'I'm your surrogate father.'

'Father! We never think of you that way. I thought you knew. We couldn't stop you changing our names.'

'But you wouldn't object to the Army. I've a cousin in high places who'd put in a word.'

'No,' Boyce conceded ungraciously. 'I'd not mind being a soldier.'

'Then, why all the bluster?'

'It's Mama who should say!'

'Very well, then.' Barney was relying on the new, softer Erin to range herself on his side.

There was a pause. 'Barney is quite right. It would do you good to have to obey someone else. These continual quarrels tire me. You'll soon see what side your bread's buttered. When I think of the past!'

The triumph vanished from Boyce's face. 'Mama!'

'And while we are about it, do you not think that Sebastian would benefit from being sent to some good boarding-school? He hangs about you like a girl, Erin. I intended to mention this some time ago but it's still not too late.'

Sebastian had turned the colour of chalk. He sat still and straight, saying nothing.

'You really think, Barney—?'

'I do, Erin. It's for the child's good. Someone must break the cord. Let it be me.'

'Very well. But it must be somewhere Sebastian will be happy—'

'Of course he'll be happy. Why shouldn't he be?'

'Then, when you've got rid of us all, you'll be able to devote yourself to Charlotte,' Boyce said loudly. 'That's what you've always wanted, Kerruish, isn't it.

Mama to yourself and that plain lump of your begetting. Thank God there were no others. One such is enough—'

Barney's face turned dreadfully white. There was no mistaking the depth of the wound Boyce had inflicted. Kerruish raised his head and stared at them. Erin so like her daughter, Sebastian who looked at nothing, Boyce whose face blazed with temper and the beginnings of belated discomfiture.

'Boyce!' Erin sprang to her feet, her eyes hard as emerald. 'You can go after your troublesome sister and try to keep your tongue under control.' She struck his cheek hard.

Sebastian rose to his feet and made his way blindly from the dining-room. Boyce clattered after him, his colour high and fists clenched.

Charlotte had not moved since the trouble began. Her brown, undistinguished face reflected nothing. But she would never forgive Boyce. Never— She hated him dreadfully.

Erin burst into tears. For years now, she had glossed over the cracks in their relationships, but this one supper-party had laid everything bare. And on top of it all, Barney was going to Liverpool just when she needed him.

'I've had enough to eat, Papa,' Charlotte said evenly. 'May I go, please?'

'If you wish, my dear. Sleep well.' Barney managed to smile.

'Good night.'

'As if she could sleep well after all that,' Erin murmured and drank some more claret with indecent haste. 'Boyce was very cruel.' Like his Irish landowning grandfather, she thought. Blood will out.

'Forget them. It's growing pains they're experiencing and I'd not have you hurt while they endure them.' The pallor had receded and he looked more like himself.

'But, they're so young—'

'My dear, I was working like a Trojan at their age. It's done me no harm. Has it?'

She looked at him, seeing not the wide mouth and the round face, the stoutish body, but the generosity that was reflected from his gaze. Erin shook her head mutely.

'Well, now that we're alone, how would you feel about coming with me? For the honeymoon we never had? You've never been to Liverpool, have you. We'll have more time now that the boys are to be off our hands, to take a trip now and again. We'll go to Glasgow next year and Cumberland the year after. They say the Lakes are very fine and I'd like to show you off. I'm still more than proud of you. And there's London—'

'I thought—you were not going to take me. You mentioned only yourself.'

'As if I would go anywhere without you.'

'I'll need some clothes.' The old Erin reasserted herself, if a little shakily.

'I'll arrange everything, then.'

'Oh, Barney—' Her eyes shone.

He sat there for a moment, wanting her to say that she loved him, but she did not. He'd like to have heard her say it just once. But how could she? It was only in fairy tales that the princess fell in love with the beast. He must be content with what he had.

Liverpool was quite unknown to Erin. The squalor round the docks reminded her of Dublin, smells and tumbledown warehouses, beggars and whores. But the main streets were smarter and some of the hotels would take your breath away.

Barney's friends, George and Muriel Bascombe, had recommended the Chatham Hotel, named after William Pitt who died in the year it was completed.

Erin loved the opulence of its main rooms, the fine plasterwork and fireplaces. The rich hangings and draped beds. The tasty, substantial meals that kept Barney in good humour and forever dipping into his pocket. Her new pleasure in his attentions hadn't stopped her magpie acquisitiveness.

They had driven about the growing city, looking their fill on the wide, silver thoroughfare of the river with the moon glimmering on it in ribbons of gold.

Later, in their room, the curtains drawn around their bed, Barney, a little tipsy with over-indulgence at supper, told Erin at last of the disappointment that beset him.

'I think—I hope—you do have some affection for me, lass, haven't you?'

She looked up at him, her hair distractingly lovely in the lamplight. Barney had always liked to watch her when he made love.

'Of course I do. More so lately.'

'That's what I thought. Then why—why when we had no trouble begetting Charlotte, can't I get another child on you?'

She smiled at him a little warily. 'How do I know the answer to that? I'm not God.'

'Erin!'

'Perhaps—it's me age.' She relapsed, defensively, into her old accent.

'You're not that old. I know you still have your monthlies. How could I not? But there's been nothing. Not even a miss. And Charlotte came straight away.'

'Does it mean so much to you?' She drew his head to her breast, enjoying the weight of his body against her own. Damn Boyce for making him remember that blighted hope.

'More than anything I can think of, except losing you. Never leave me—'

'As if I would.' To think that he'd hugged the disappointment to himself all these years. She was conscious of an unexpected pang.

'I want a son of my own,' he whispered and began to kiss her warm flesh. The effect was delicious. All those years of sterility and then this new feeling. Why couldn't she? Would it be so terrible? The others had been so easy. But now she was much older and they were almost fully grown apart from Charlotte. Who was plain and characterless and whom she'd always secretly detested. If she'd had Barney's warmth and appreciation, it might be different, but she hadn't. Charlotte was cold as spring water and as stiff as a broom handle.

'No one can say we haven't tried.'

'No, love,' Barney admitted. 'You've been a good wife. None better.'

But had she! Erin was aware of her own duplicities and shortcomings as never before. Guiltily, she held him the closer, whispering, 'Try again, then. Who knows, the change of air could work wonders.'

But when he was done with her, she rose and took a spoonful of the draught she always kept at her bedside.

'What's that?' Barney asked sleepily.

'Only a draught for indigestion. Must have been those chops, love.'

He thought nothing of it. She'd been taking the stuff for years. Perhaps she should see a doctor?

He'd forgotten it in the morning, Erin enchantingly sleepy beside him, her lashes covering half of her cheeks. She snuggled up against him. He kissed her shoulder gratefully.

After breakfast he gave her a purseful of coins, telling her to buy herself some pretties. 'I will benefit as well as you. I enjoy seeing you well-dressed.'

'Barney. I don't deserve you!'

'I'm glad we're both pleased. I'll be engaged on business till supper. Till then, my sweet.'

Erin spent a halcyon day. She felt cosseted and conscious of her own fortune. And the shops were so enticing with their trinkets and silks and gauze. She bought a walking-dress and feathered hat though what Castletown folk would make of it she couldn't say! The thought made her laugh. Then there was the ivory fan and the length of muslin and the bonnet shaped like a Greek helmet. If her hair was cut short at the front and sides—

She experimented with the scissors when she got back to the Chatham and was pleased with the result. The new style took years off her age.

Barney was not alone when he returned. With him was a squarish young man with devastatingly honest eyes and little to say for himself.

'This is Nat Gelling, my dear. I've seen half a dozen possibles today and Nat beat them all.'

Nat Gelling shook hands with her, almost crushing her fingers, his eyes on the new curls that framed her face.

He looked at her hair all through the meal and Erin was flattered. Men always stared at her crowning glory.

'All of my children are red-haired,' she told him.

'Not all. Charlotte isn't,' Barney said.

'I'd forgotten her.' It was astonishing how often the thought of Charlotte escaped her. 'How stupid of me.'

'Elizabeth's her mother's image,' Barney told his new engineer.

Erin thought the young man's heavy expression lightened.

'Nat will come back with us,' Barney went on, 'so you'll find a corner for him until he gets settled, won't you, love.'

'I daresay that can be arranged.'

'Oh, I couldn't impose. . . .'

'Why not?' Erin challenged. 'Barney's very self-willed. If he's made up his mind. . . .' But all the time she was the one deferred to. Worshipped. . . . She smiled.

'You're not wed?' Barney asked the serious young man. Nat shook his head and the strong shoulders strained against the sober material of his coat.

'Plenty of bonny lasses on Man,' he was assured by a comfortable host.

What was the poor creature supposed to say to that, Erin thought indulgently?

Barney poured them all more claret and this had the effect of livening Gelling up considerably. He could like Elizabeth, Erin thought, if he was so struck on red hair. But she had her sights on something better for her daughter and there was plenty of time.

Life had taken on a gloss and a wonderful new meaning. She was cherished, she who'd worked in the fields and been beaten regularly by her father. Barney'd go mad if he knew how she'd been treated, to what ends she'd been driven. Thank God it hadn't ruined her looks. The joy of knowing that never again would she need to humiliate herself before a man. If she didn't love Barney it was as close as she'd ever get to any real feeling.

She accepted a glass of wine and it worked deliciously on her senses, blurring the memory of her sons left behind in Castletown. Nobody would ever be able to deny Boyce anything. He was the sort to get on in the world but he wouldn't be stupid enough to get entangled with the wrong sort of woman. There was more of herself in Boyce than his easy-going, easily deterred father. Dermot O'Neill had been as weak as water, but so fascinating. Boyce had the same aura, but there was steel underneath. He'd make a beautiful soldier and end up, sure as night turned to day, a general.

Erin required another glass before she decided that Barney was indeed right about Sebastian. He was a mother's boy and would be better off getting used to a more manly way of life. He and Elizabeth could change places and no one would be any the wiser. Yes, Sebastian would take readily to the monasticism of a large school of the right kind. He'd become a man of letters, might even become a churchman or a man of law. A Member of Parliament!

Man was too small a place for her boys with their potential. When she was older she'd be basking in reflected glory, of that she hadn't the slightest doubt. Elizabeth would most certainly marry well. Power and money would be her goal. There was no sickly, sweet-missishness about Jesse's daughter. She had his toughness without the gentleness, her mother's shrewdness. Perhaps she'd have been better off with a sister?

But she had a sister. Of sorts. Unconsciously, Erin's face took on a tighter look, her mouth drawn in so that it radiated tiny, unwanted lines. Charlotte was of no consequence. She'd never do anything more riveting than scowling in some corner over a dry-as-dust book. She'd end up having to wear spectacles, the silly girl, a born spinster.

Yet, Charlotte was the daughter of a well-known and well-off man. Even her dowdiness need not preclude a marriage that would link the Kerruishes with some substantial family from Douglas. The town thrived so while Castletown had begun to stagnate.

Erin became aware that she was required to answer something that Barney and Nat Gelling had said. It was safest to smile whole-heartedly and shrug her still pretty shoulders in a gesture that could just as easily mean no as yes. Barney's eyes reflected the love she still could not wholly believe. Surely no woman was ever meant to be so happy? And he need never know why she didn't conceive. She needn't hurt him. Ever. She'd look as regretful as himself when nothing happened.

Barney replenished their glasses and a wonderful hot savoury smell presaged the imminent arrival of the welcome meal. He leaned back, content. Gelling must surely prove to be a gift from Heaven. He couldn't believe his own luck. And his heart still turned over when he looked at the woman to whom he was married. If they'd been alone he'd have wanted to take her upstairs right at this moment and to the devil with convention. Business was beginning to boom; he'd decided how best to dispose of Erin's boys in ways that would benefit them as well as himself. There would be more time to spare for Charlotte, a daughter of whom any man could be justly proud. Plenty of brains in that externally ordinary-looking head. Deep, Charlotte was, but he could feel her love for him. She'd not change. And now that Erin was so loving, there could still be the realisation of his dream. His own boy.

'You'll stay with us, then, till you find your feet?' he repeated to young Gelling.

'If you don't mind.'

'Nay, lad. We'll get to know one another.'

Erin smiled her acquiescence, knowing they both admired the picture she presented in her best green gown.

Barney had begun to talk about Nat's future duties and describe the mine that bore her name, and now Gelling was in his element, eager and bright-eyed, his shyness gone.

Their talk washed around Erin like a benevolent tide. Mines were money and wealth meant comfort and position for them all. Slowly her mind turned to the striped muslin. The white and green would please Barney. Dear frog prince. . . .

* * *

Karran thought she would die as she saw Hugh usher the children up the gangplank. But it was only a temporary pain. By the time they stood by the rail and waved to her she was quite composed again. Joseph and Dinah would be perfectly all right. They had their father and their grandparents. Meg looked so unlike herself in a plain coat and bonnet. She rarely covered her hair at Croggan and then only with a shawl.

It seemed such a small vessel to go all the way to America. It couldn't be true! But it was. The ropes were all flung off and the board taken down. The gap between the quay and the ship grew wider and the pain leapt again so that Karran gasped and blinked away hot tears. Dinah was fluttering her best handkerchief.

Their faces receded alarmingly fast. Now she only recognised them by the colours of the clothes they wore and the little white speck that fluttered still. Then there was only the shape of the ship growing smaller and smaller until it was like the three-masted schooner inside the glass bottle that had belonged to Jesse Kinrade.

She turned away when she could see no more, heartsore and a little lost. But she wasn't alone. Howard, sensing that she'd rather stay at the quay by herself, had arranged to meet her at the Schooner Hotel after she said her goodbyes. Howard was a rock to hold on to.

He saw her come into the entrance hall, her face very pale against the dark red coat. It was the same shade as that gipsy-looking jacket she'd worn when he first knew her. But, oh, the difference in the child. With her hair tamed and a dusting of rice-powder to tone down the skin, the new elegance, she was every inch the young lady. Had they spoiled her? There had been a raw magnetism about the original Karran, the sort of splendour he'd seen in Italian peasants and not displeasing. An earthiness that was undeniably exciting. Was it gone?

They had tea and crumpets by the fire and bit by bit, the dark shadows round her eyes were smoothed away. She described the ship's departure and the look of strain did not come back. She would think of them all, but now that she could not see them any more the sadness wouldn't return. It was bad to look back into the past. It hadn't done anyone she knew any good.

'Ready?' John Howard asked. 'Ready to go home?'

Her eyes widened and brightened into pieces of shining jet. Howard had never seen such black eyes on another living person. Her young profile was so proud. No. She had not changed fundamentally.

'Home?'

'That's what I said.' He gathered up his stick and gloves.

'What happens if I do anything wrong? Will I be expected to leave?'

'I can't visualise—'

'No, but imagine I did. No one would expect you to be responsible for me. Another man's child.'

199

'My dear Karran, it would have to be something unforgivable for me to cast you off.'

'But what about Mrs. Howard? Couldn't she turn against me as she did against that girl, Kate?'

'Isn't this all too hypothetical, my dear?'

'My father wasn't at all a good person. People change— Blood will come out.'

'I refuse to listen to any more. I shouldn't brood about things one can't alter. We want you to be our daughter. You've had an upsetting day and that's why you are suddenly filled with doubts and fears. It's to be expected. Give yourself another few weeks and it will seem as if you have always lived at Ravensdowne.'

'Yes. You're perfectly right.' Karran squared her shoulders and raised her head. 'Everything has been very strange but it isn't going to stay that way. How long have I got before I lose the bet we made?'

'Three months.'

'Will we have time for a lesson when we get back tonight?

'I fear not.'

'Very well. I'm ready.' She took his arm and they stepped out into the windswept street.

Karran noticed the harbour light but never realised the significance it had for her. She had not heard of Lily and Joseph or baby Samuel or the loss of a hundred and more fishing-boats one night when Nature had gone mad. She thought how prettily the gleam shivered on the water, like the moonlight around Shag Rock, and a deep, wild excitement took possession of her.

* * *

She lay wide awake. It was not dark, now that her eyes had grown accustomed to the night and faint traces of moonlight laid patinas of palest silver on the face of the mirror and the backs of the silver brushes.

John had been so kind about the transfer of herself from one world to another. He'd understood when she wanted to ride back to Croggan on occasion, but she recognised the relief he was unable to hide on her return. It was as though he did not quite believe that she was now his and Emily's. Yet she was quite certainly his.

The thought of Emily was never so welcome. Karran could not think why there was that reservation on her own part, but no one could make themselves feel true warmth where there was none. But she would play her part of pretending that Emily was just as dear as John. She couldn't hurt John and he was as steady as a rock where she herself was concerned. In her heart she recognised that he'd never forsake her however bad she was. Not that she meant to be. God forbid!

She was to be secure, to become educated far beyond the level of most other persons. How privileged she was! Sometimes it seemed that it must all vanish like fairy gold. She need never bow her head when she saw the Kerruishes. The same tragedy that had touched her had visited Erin Kerruish and could be never flung in her face like a weapon, for all her aunt's airs and graces.

The smell of lavender stole out of the pillowcase like a ghost. They were all to live happily ever after. Hugh and Meg would contrive to let her know how they fared in America. Their news would be filled with excitement. Deep inside herself Karran realised that she would have welcomed the challenge of an unknown country if it had not been for her bond with John Howard. She'd never meet anyone else with whom she'd have such an affinity. Was it wicked to be glad that poverty seemed gone for good? She'd have loved John without the fine trappings.

Tomorrow she'd have to work especially hard if she were to win the bet. The letters danced in front of her eyes. K.K.—K.K. The initials would change one day. She wondered what they would be several years hence, but the answer must remain hidden for a time.

The tide had risen and the water slopped around the Shag Rock. Her happiness was one with the moonshine and the soft splash of the sea.

PRINCESS DAISY
by Judith Krantz

She was born Princess Marguerite Alexandrovna Valensky.
But everyone called her Daisy. She was a blonde beauty
living in a world of aristocrats and countless wealth. Her
father was a prince, a Russian nobleman. Her mother was an
American movie goddess. Men desired her. Women envied
her. Daisy's life was a fairytale filled with parties and balls,
priceless jewels, money and love. Then, suddenly, the
fairytale ended. And Princess Daisy had to start again, with
nothing. Except the secret she guarded from the day she was
born.

SBN: 0 552 11660 2   Price: £1.75

THE COMPANY OF WOMEN
by Mary Gordon

Felicitas Taylor had been raised by her widowed mother and three closest friends under the all-pervading influence of Father Cyprian, a fiercely independent Catholic priest. But his guidance was of little help when she finally gained independence. In a desperate search for love and acceptance from her peers, she became the object of a brutal and far-reaching lesson in seduction and betrayal. Only then could Felicitas find her true self and her place in the world.

0 552 12001 4   £1.75

A WORLD FULL OF STRANGERS
by Cynthia Freeman

The story of a family you'll never forget! A rich, dramatic saga of passion and love, of sin and retribution, spanning three generations of family life—from the ghettos of New York to the glittering hills of San Francisco. . . .

DAVID   who destroyed his past to live a life of power and glory.

KATIE   who lived with her past, whose roots and memories were too deep for her ever to be able to forget.

MARK   their son, who had the courage to struggle towards the sacred heritage his father had denied him.

MAGGIE   the successful and glamorous woman David wanted because she was everything Katie was not.

SBN: 0 552 11775 7   Price: £1.95

ZEMINDAR
  by Valerie Fitzgerald

To Laura Hewitt, India was an exciting challenge—an India of extravagant princes, of the British Raj, of the first rumblings of disquiet and tension smouldering silently from state to state.

Laura had travelled there as the companion of her indulged newly-wed cousin Emily—trying, on the journey to suppress both her love for Charles, and her resentment of Emily who had stolen Charles from her.

Their destination was the kingdom of Oudh, to the vast zemindar estate of Charles's unknown brother, Oliver Erskine. And even before Laura had set foot on land she heard tales, rumours, conjecture about Oliver Erskine, the ZEMINDAR.

0 552 99019 1   £2.50

A KIND OF LOVING
by Stan Barstow

This first book of the Vic Brown trilogy portrays the way in which young Vic comes to terms—the hard way—with adult life and his feelings for the beautiful but demanding Ingrid.

Hard-hitting and down-to-earth, Stan Barstow's novel deals with ordinary people and their problems—the people of a close-knit, working-class community.

Now acknowledged as a classic of modern literature, this bestselling novel is as alive and as relevant today, as when it was first published in 1960.

SBN: 0 552 11805 2   Price: £1.50

THE RIGHT TRUE END
by Stan Barstow

As a divorced man, Vic has made it on his own terms in London. A prize job, a flash car and as much sex as he can handle . . . but it's still not enough.

Ten years ago, with Donna, he knew he had something real, the way things should be between a man and a woman. Something so bloody marvellous that when she walks back into his life again, Vic's scared to death he'll mess up his chances the second time round . . .

SBN: 0 552 11808 7   Price: £1.50

A SELECTED LIST OF FINE NOVELS
IN CORGI PAPERBACK

☐ 11682 3	A BROTHER'S TALE	*Stan Barstow*	£1.50
☐ 11805 2	A KIND OF LOVING	*Stan Barstow*	£1.50
☐ 11807 9	WATCHERS ON THE SHORE	*Stan Barstow*	£1.50
☐ 11808 7	THE RIGHT TRUE END	*Stan Barstow*	£1.50
☐ 99019 1	ZEMINDAR	*Valerie Fitzgerald*	£2.50
☐ 12043 X	PRIMA DONNA	*Nancy Freedman*	£1.50
☐ 11730 7	PORTRAITS	*Cynthia Freeman*	£1.95
☐ 11776 5	FAIRYTALES	*Cynthia Freeman*	£1.95
☐ 11925 3	COME POUR THE WINE	*Cynthia Freeman*	£1.75
☐ 11775 7	A WORLD FULL OF STRANGERS	*Cynthia Freeman*	£1.95
☐ 11852 4	DAYS OF WINTER	*Cynthia Freeman*	£1.95
☐ 11140 6	FINAL PAYMENTS	*Mary Gordon*	£1.00
☐ 12001 4	THE COMPANY OF WOMEN	*Mary Gordon*	£1.75
☐ 11660 2	PRINCESS DAISY	*Judith Krantz*	£1.75
☐ 11207 0	TAMARISK	*Claire Lorrimer*	£1.25
☐ 11726 9	CHANTAL	*Claire Lorrimer*	£1.95
☐ 11959 8	THE CHATELAINE	*Claire Lorrimer*	£1.95
☐ 11957 1	RELENTLESS STORM	*Claire Lorrimer*	£1.25
☐ 10584 8	MAVREEN	*Claire Lorrimer*	£1.95